Youthful
Indulgence

Youthful Indulgence

Thomas E. Coughlin

Fitzgerald & LaChapelle Publishing

Written, produced and printed in the United States of America

ISBN: 978-0-9666202-9-0

Cover Design: Lisa Atkins, Pelham, New Hampshire

FIRST EDITION

Fitzgerald & LaChapelle Publishing
P.O. Box 352
Chester, NH   03036-0352
Phone: (603) 463-8300   Email: chestercpa@yahoo.co

Acknowledgements

Dick and Sherri Varano of Billy's Chowder House, Carol and Bruce at the Beachcomber and the Hunters of the Wells IGA Supermarket. Amy McAfee, Betsy Chase. The good people at the Mott House in Kennebunkport where a tour of that grand, old mansion gave me the physical layout for my fictitious Bruckner House.

Introduction

Readers will certainly observe that my latest work of fiction, *Youthful Indulgence,* is approximately half the size of my previous books. This came about purely from the story lines I decided upon about a year ago and not from some grand scheme on my part. For the longest time I've wanted to write a romantic story that explored the psychological obstacles that a man and woman might face in a May/December romance. My desire to write a novel or novella with this set of circumstances was intensified when, over the last couple of years, I came in direct, personal contact with individuals who were engaged in such a relationship. Sometime during this period, I decided to break from the more common roles of the genders and make the female character the older of the two lovers.

In writing fiction, I have always tried to avoid story lines that required the reader to accept premises and facts that flirted with the unimaginable. *Youthful Indulgence* was no exception. To this end, I only had to harken back to my own days as a bachelor in my twenties. With a constant eye out for the ladies, I found myself, on occasion, admiring the physicality of women a generation older than me. Hence, I reasoned that it was not some crazy notion for a twenty-two-year old male to become attracted to an attractive, physically fit woman in her forties.

The time line of *Youthful Indulgence* covers less than four months in the life of the recently divorced, Marion Bell. It is set in 2002 so I had to be careful not to bring technology into the novella that was not in existence at that time. The subject matter and the brief time line over which it plays dictated how many pages I had to tell the story.

From the day I first put pen to paper and decided to write fiction, I have shied away from writing horror and gore. I have always thought if fiction writing were a tree then fiction writers of horror must certainly occupy the lower branches. It seemed to me that, just as comedians lace their sets with more and more profanity to spice up their routines, so then would writers of horror become more and more gory and grotesque to entertain their readers. I wanted no part of that charade. However, about a year ago, a story came to me that was neither unduly gory nor grotesque but could take readers to a dark, dark place. It was at that time that the story of *Little Henrietta* began to take form.

Little Henrietta comes with the standard ingredients of many ghost and horror stories, an old, sprawling mansion and things that go bump in the night. However, I believe it is the addition of a third, unconventional element that takes it to a place where so many other ghost stories have failed to go. Interestingly, the most difficult thing in writing this short story was coming up with a thought-provoking and constant interior to the haunted mansion. Following a period of some struggle, this obstacle was addressed when I had the good fortune to wander into the Mott House in downtown Kennebunkport and took a tour of the building. Five minutes into the tour, I knew I had the interior for my fictional Bruckner House. Once equipped with a mental map of rooms for my fictional mansion, it was a reasonably easy task to move my characters, both the living and the dead, through the rooms and toward an epiphany.

Tom Coughlin

Chapter 1

Fingers of estuary water glistened while curling around Billy's Chowder House, an iconic restaurant seemingly adrift in the middle of the Rachel Carson Wildlife Sanctuary. The sun's glare prompted Marion Bell to snatch her sunglasses from above the car's visor and perch them on the bridge of her nose. Her journey nearly over, she peered into the distance in the general direction of her oceanfront home at Wells Beach in the hope of catching an early glimpse of the house. Her effort proved to be an exercise in futility given the almost unbroken line of classical, early twentieth century beach homes and modern monstrosities lining the west side of Atlantic Avenue.

Marion Bell was making the first visit to her beach property since acquiring it through her recent divorce's division of assets. Four hours earlier she had bid farewell to her old life and watched the State of Connecticut blur into the past tense in her car's rearview mirror. Now, she was about to write the next chapter of her life here on the southern coast of Maine, she thought. Directly ahead of her at the end of Mile Road was the modest cluster of shops serving the beach. It only took seconds for her Toyota to reach the edge of the parking lot on the lip of the Atlantic Ocean. Reaching the small group of commercial buildings, the forty-seven-year-old's spirits lifted as she observed signs of life behind the windows of the Beachcomber, the village's primary gift shop. It was comforting to know that some things had not changed in the past year while her life crashed and burned around her. Turning onto Atlantic Avenue, she caught sight of the store owner of the shop stocking shelves by the window. Memorial Day weekend was only three weeks away and with it came the start of the tourist season. Marion focused her eyes back on the road and drove the half mile northward to her residence.

She reached the house and pulled into its parking area. Looking up, she caught sight of the words, *The Good Life,* neatly painted onto a placard over the garage door. The irony was not lost on her, eliciting a short burst of laughter. The front of the property carried signs of the winter's blowing sand, not to mention stones brought up by surging tidewater. Turning off the car's engine, she leaned back in the driver's seat and stared up at the house. So much had transpired in her life since her last visit to Maine, she thought. Her mind harkened back to the previous May and Maureen's visit. Maureen Brady had been her best friend since the fourth grade and the two had spent the third week in May of 2001 not only cementing but building upon their friendship. They had come together here at Wells Beach at a time when both faced an individual crisis in their lives and emerged stronger from

13

the experience. Marion took in a deep breath and felt reality take hold of her. How could either of them have foreseen in their wildest dreams the nightmare scenario of the World Trade Center less than four months later. Marion pushed her memories of that dreadful day to the back of her mind, not willing to mentally relive the call from the Brady family on the fate of her lifelong friend. Marion was a tall woman, standing just over five feet, nine inches. She was pretty but never considered beautiful, even in her youth. Her sharp, facial features gave the world notice of her intelligence. After reaching the age of forty, her jet-black hair had given way to streaks of silver. Not unexpectedly, it was a look many professional men, unless completely obsessed with youth, found attractive. She entered her cottage through the garage door and climbed a narrow set of stairs toward the kitchen. Reaching the first floor she was shocked by its Spartan appearance. A few weeks before she had allowed her ex-husband to visit their summer home and remove anything carrying an emotional attachment. At first glance, it appeared his sentimentality extended to everything from small appliances to pots and pans. Except for major appliances, nothing seemed to have survived his sense of nostalgia.

"Good old Monty, a total asshole to the very end," she thought. Moving into the kitchen, she inspected the cupboards and saw a few food items had survived, coffee, non-dairy creamer and a box of instant soup mix to name a few. She swung out the refrigerator door and observed a handful of cans of Moxie stacked inside. She was, without question, back in Maine, she reasoned. She snatched a can of soda and strolled to the oceanside of the house. Collapsing onto a chair, she snapped open her soda and peered in the direction of the Atlantic Ocean.

Marion threw back her head, attempting to remember her last visit to the house. Within seconds, she came up with the second or third week of November, just a little ahead of Thanksgiving. It was about that time when she began picking up on small inconsistencies in her husband's work schedule and overnight travel plans. Then, a couple of weeks before Christmas came the talk. It was on a Friday night. Mia, their nineteen-year-old daughter, was on an overnight with a female friend. Monty had the stage set for his exit speech and it was delivered in perfect form. From start to finish it took under three minutes, she recollected. Marion had sat speechless during the entire process, thinking she would awaken at any moment and breathe a sigh of relief. However, his well-rehearsed discourse ended and with no time for cross-examination or rebuttal. Unknown to her, his luggage was packed and loaded in the family SUV, allowing her husband of over twenty years to effortlessly turn and walk out of her life. Her eyes dropped to the floor while she drove the bitter memory from the prior December from her consciousness. Following a brief pause, she remembered the two bottles of wine purchased in New Hampshire earlier in the day and traced her steps back to the car.

By early in the afternoon, Marion had removed the porch furniture from the cellar and returned it to its place overlooking the sand and pebbles of Wells Beach.

She had no plans to think about her employment picture let alone search for a position over the next few months. Plucking a wine glass from a kitchen cabinet, she strolled through the living room with chardonnay bottle in hand and made her way back to the porch. The air was far from warm but, nonetheless, she kicked off her shoes and seated herself, propping her feet up on the porch railing. The beach was, for the most part, free of human beings. She glanced over at the empty, adjacent chair and thought of Maureen. She remembered standing in front of the television set on that September morning and watching the first tower, seemingly in slow motion, collapse upon itself. In an act of self-preservation, she focused her mind back on her surroundings and took a sip from her glass of wine.

At present, the tide was out. Marion's mind flashed to more palatable matters. Her finances were currently strong. Her severance package back in February had seen to that. At present, her plan was to lounge around the beach until the very end of September before putting herself back in gear and re-entering the job market. Thoughts of her personal finances jolted her memory back to that Friday afternoon in February. Snow had been forecasted for Hartford and she had been playing with the idea of cutting out early. It had not been a productive day as she recalled, her mind had repeatedly been dragged from the work at hand by thoughts and images of Monty frolicking with the twenty-three-year-old child who had taken her place in their bed. Nothing tortured her more than imagining the sexual activity between her nearly fifty-year-old ex-husband and the young trollop who had taken possession of him, body and soul, a year earlier. Marion had been tormenting herself with these thoughts over the better part of that fateful, February day when she was called into Steve Cortez's office. She had always had a decent relationship with the man just above her on the corporate food chain. He had appeared uncharacteristically uncomfortable on this day, shuffling papers atop his desk and failing to make eye contact. Interestingly, she thought back to a business trip taken together ten years earlier and the sexual advance by him she was forced to rebuff. Watching him fidget in his chair that day, she was sure he was about to reintroduce the proposition. That was until he lifted his eyes and stared directly at her.

"For budgetary reasons, finance, sales, marketing and the human resources departments have been ordered to shed someone from payroll. Marion, I'm afraid you didn't make the cut," he blurted out before dropping his eyes back to the surface of his desk. The words cut through her like the point of a sword. She had never seen it coming. In gangster lingo, she had taken two in the hat. Dumbstruck by the announcement, she sat in a state of stunned shock before bursting into tears. It was a reaction foreign to her. He jumped up from his chair and joined her on the leather couch where she was seated.

"It's okay Steve. I'm fine," she reassured him. She had emotionally collapsed under the weight of an accumulation of events.

Marion rose from her chair and stepped up to the porch railing. She inhaled a gust of sea air blowing in from the Atlantic and strained her eyes toward the horizon. This would be her summer of healing, she thought. Taking a sip from her wine glass, she turned and looked southward. The oceanside windows on the Sullivan house next door were still boarded up. She dreaded their arrival this year and the awkward explanation of the divorce. Jerry and May were always closer to Monty than to her, she reasoned. It was Monty who had brought the cottage into the marriage. He had all the boyhood memories of Wells Beach, not her. She had already ruled out trying to avoid them. Their houses and open porches were practically identical and no more than twelve feet apart. Thoughts of the approaching summer brought the last nail in her emotional coffin to mind. Following her last final exam, her daughter, Mia, would be joining her father in Connecticut and working the summer in the Hartford area. Her daughter's decision, it was explained, had nothing to do with prior commitments or a budding romance. It was a matter of parental compatibility. Marion felt an attack of depression coming on. She retreated to the car and unloaded three suitcases of clothing, accessories and cosmetics. After dragging her luggage up the narrow stairwell to the main floor, she changed into a more athletic outfit and made for the beach, leaving her sneakers by the porch entrance to the house.

The walk alongside the advancing and retreating, blue water proved beneficial. She felt her depressed feelings recede and be replaced by a sense of subdued optimism. She took inventory of herself. She had long considered one hundred and thirty-five pounds to be her ideal weight. She had tipped the scales at one hundred and forty-six pounds two days earlier. Eleven pounds was nothing, she thought. She decided to put herself on the Atkins Diet the following day. The diet and two to three miles of vigorous walking a day could bring her down to her perfect weight by mid-June, she suspected. Marion's meditative walk on this first day took her to the jetty and then southward to the edge of Fisherman's Cove. Nowhere was the beach crowded but on those occasions when she did encounter other individuals, they were mostly in pairs. In the past, whether on business or personal travel, she had no problem with the solitary life or the appearance of being alone. There was always the knowledge that she had a husband and a daughter at home to psychologically prop her up. That was before and now she lived in a new reality. For this reason, she seemed to be overly aware of the glances from those she passed on the ocean's edge. She wondered if she wore any outward evidence of her solitary life. Marion was sure she was far more attractive than a majority of women her age but this did nothing to alleviate a dampening sense of insecurity. Her future diet and exercise were not enough, she decided. She would remove the gray from her hair and return it to jet black. Arriving back at the house, she climbed the stairs to her bedroom and began the arduous task of unpacking for the summer.

Chapter 2

It was day four of Marion's life adventure on the southern coast of Maine. Outside, the air was unseasonably cold with a forecast of temperatures peaking in the middle fifties. Tucked warmly beneath her bed covers, she thought back to a sound that awakened her sometime around midnight. It was the slamming of a car door and she was quite sure it had come from the Sullivan's property. The sound of multiple car doors closing had been followed by the expected shuffling of footsteps but little else. Marion checked the clock on her night table. It was precisely nine o'clock. Elevating her body off the mattress, she caught sight of the ocean where whitecaps dotted the water's surface. Staring absentmindedly out her bedroom window for the next minute, she picked up on a few speckles of water on the glass before the sound of raindrops were audible. Searching for some incentive to start her day, she remembered it was day three of her diet and she was anxious to check her weight on the downstairs, bathroom scale. Wrapping herself in a bathrobe, she scurried down the flight of stairs and into the bathroom. She was pleased with the results. She weighed in at one hundred and forty-four pounds, a loss of two pounds in two days. She stepped in front of the bathroom mirror and eyed her head of thick, black hair. Her revitalization program was up and going, she thought.

Following a breakfast of bacon and eggs, Marion stepped out onto the cottage porch with coffee cup in hand. Dressed in a loosely fitting sweatshirt and pants, she huddled onto a chair and sipped on her beverage. Wells Beach had few walkers on this morning owing to the cool temperature, light rain and a gusty wind. On this day, she hoped to come up with an itinerary of activities to get her out of the house. Thus far, she had only left the protection of her four walls to shop for groceries at the IGA or walk the sometime sandy, sometimes rocky beach at the back of her house. The idea of sitting in a restaurant alone was still a peak too high to climb at this stage. She was enjoying a long sip from her coffee cup when the sound of work from the Sullivan house grabbed her attention. She stood up and walked to the porch railing. A short distance away, a man was removing the boards from the oceanside windows. It wasn't Jerry. Jerry was prematurely grey. The male turned in her direction. It was Jimmy Sullivan, their son. The young man walked to his tool box and removed a small crowbar. He also caught sight of her.

"Hey, good morning Mrs. Bell," he called over to her. She flashed him a smile. "I waited until after nine to make any noise. The contractors start at seven if I'm not mistaken," he explained.

"Your thoughtfulness is appreciated," she called back. "Let me know if I can be of any help," she offered graciously, more out of something to say than anything.

"Does that include coffee?" asked the young man. "My folks left me nothing here and I mean nothing," he reiterated. "I didn't expect milk or bread or anything like that. But damn it, not even a jar of instant coffee or a can of soup." The young man's response caught her by surprise. She instructed him to give her a few minutes to start another pot and invited him to join her on the porch in ten minutes.

Jimmy Sullivan had already made himself comfortable on her porch by the time Marion brought two steaming cups of coffee outside. Jimmy was a handsome kid, just under six feet in height, in good, physical condition and with a shock of auburn hair that he wore beyond average length. His face retained a few lingering freckles from his younger years but it was his smile that she found most appealing. He jumped to his feet when she joined him outside. There was an old-world quality to his gesture that both surprised and pleased her. Placing down the tray, she pointed to a handful of small, oatmeal cookies for his consideration. He snatched one and shoved it into him mouth.

"Are you short of money?" Marion asked. Her question sent him into a gale of laughter.

"For God's sake no," he roared back. "It's just a case of getting in too late last night and being too lazy to get off my ass this morning," he explained. He reached for a second cookie and inhaled the aroma from his coffee.

"I feel terrible for not being able to offer you something more substantial. I just went on the Atkins's Diet a couple of days ago so unless you want a side of beef or a whole chicken I'm in a bad position to play the good neighbor," she explained. He sipped on his coffee and took in her words. A puzzled look broke over his face.

"And why would you be on a diet?" he asked in a serious tone. She suspected he was being something less than sincere.

"Because I'm eleven, I'm sorry, nine pounds overweight," she answered. "If I wasn't in these clothes that are hanging off me, you would see what I'm talking about."

"My God, nine pounds is nothing, Mrs. Bell," he insisted. "I can honestly say that, out of all of my parent's friends, you are the last one who should be on a diet."

"So, when can I expect your folks to arrive?" Marion asked, eager to remove her weight from the conversation.

"You can't. They'll pretty much be skipping Wells this year. With all of the terrorism warnings going up they got a great deal on an extended tour of Europe." She looked at him curiously.

"Aren't you scheduled to get married this summer or am I getting you mixed up with someone else? The years bring on memory problems," she joked. The young man's mood grew serious.

"No, that was me but it's off. Melissa got cold feet. You see, Melissa got an incredible job offer out in San Francisco and she got cold feet," he reported. "To be completely honest, I think it had more to do with San Francisco than her cold feet," he confessed.

"Better before than after you're settled down together," quipped Marion.

"That's what I keep telling myself. It's just one tough break in a shit year that seemed to consist of nothing but tough breaks. You probably remember my folks bragging about the job I was recruited for last October. Well, that went up in smoke over the winter. It seems that annual earnings went in the toilet at Kearsarge-Bidwell in 2001 and hiring was cut way, way back. Consultants were brought in to bayonet the wounded and I was a casualty even before I stepped through the door. I'd say that has loser written all over it, wouldn't you?" he asked.

"Don't be silly. I'd say it was more of a case of existing management screwing up and not you," she insisted. Jimmy shook his head and continued.

"If only I was done. Hop back on the train to Loserville but watch your step," he said, playfully reaching out one hand. "Largely because of the whole Melissa fiasco, my GPA took a massive hit in my senior year. It dropped nearly thirty points over my last two semesters so I'm leaving school with no job and shaky prospects. So, my parents are happy to spend a couple of months over in Europe with me out of sight. Failure is contagious, you know."

"You'll bounce back, Jimmy. You're young and you'll bounce back," insisted Marion. She was slightly overwhelmed by the boy's candidness and even wrestled with the idea of sharing her own story.

Coffee and conversation went on for close to half an hour before Jimmy begged off and returned to his task of removing the hurricane boards from his parent's windows. Marion moved indoors. She was happy to hear of the Sullivan's plans to tour Europe. No doubt, Jimmy would eventually ask about Monty's absence but certainly not request a full, blow by blow account of the breakup as she expected his parents would. For all she knew, the Sullivans had already gotten an account of the Bell's marital crash landing. Marion retreated to the kitchen where she washed and dried the few dirty dishes. From time to time she would pick up on the sound of Jimmy working next door. There was something comforting about it, she thought. It made her feel less alone. In fact, just having someone to share coffee with on this morning lifted her spirits. She had forgotten to ask how long he would be staying in Wells.

Perfect spring weather invaded southern Maine on this weekend, Marion's first weekend at the house. She was still gun shy about dining out alone at any local restaurants but did bite the bullet and attended the movies. She timed her arrival to coincide with the lowering of the lights for the feature film. Her plan worked.

There were no more than two dozen people in the audience and she arrived with all the fanfare of a ninja warrior. Although progressing slowly she was getting the hang of the solitary life. Her Sunday morning weigh-in brought forth a pump of the fist. Her weight came in at one hundred and forty-one pounds. Marion celebrated her weight loss with four eggs for breakfast accompanied by three extra slices of bacon. She followed her morning meal with six or seven cuts of Dan Fogelberg before changing clothes for her walk. She decided to wear shorts for the first time since arriving in Maine. Her weigh-in had done wonders for her spirits and confidence.

Exiting the house in late morning, Marion turned northward, setting her sights on the Wells Harbor jetty. She decided to wear her sneakers on this day. She planned to walk the granite blocks to the end of the jetty and what she did not need was to stub a toe on the face of a protruding stone. It was only half a mile from the house to the jetty and she reached it within ten minutes. After scaling the wall of boulders, she headed eastward toward the far tip of the rocky, uneven sidewalk of stone. Her pathway was strewn with any number of potential hazards which might, at best, open a nasty gash on a victim's knee or ankle. However, Marion remained focused on the uneven rocks underfoot and made it to the harbor beacon in good time. There, she parked her back against the base to the beacon tower and took in the might and beauty of the Atlantic Ocean. Closing her eyes, she heard and felt the ocean's power surge around her as wave after wave drove up against the continent. Finally, she rose to her feet and turned her back on the sea. Inexplicably, at this moment, she felt incredibly at one with her own physicality. She drew in a breath. She was, at this moment, conscious of the half dozen pounds she had shed in the past week. She felt trimmer than she had in some time. This state of self-awareness was broken in that moment when her eyes focused on a male approaching her position on the jetty. There was nothing tentative about his movement over the surface of the granite boulders. He was running at a healthy speed given the general lack of flat surfaces. At twenty yards, Marion saw that it was Jimmy Sullivan invading her solitude.

"That's a great way to wind up with a broken neck," she called out to him. She watched as his face broke out into a grin.

"Isn't it though," he replied, making no effort to slow down. Seconds later, he reached her by the beacon where he used her body to slow his forward momentum, his hands coming to rest on her shoulders. He was out of breath. His hands remained on her for an awkward moment longer than necessary before he pulled back. Her first instinct was to admonish him for being overly familiar but she held her tongue. He smiled down sheepishly before surveying his neighbor head to toe. "Come on. Who are you kidding with all this talk about a diet?"

"Enough with the laughable flattery," she answered before pushing her way by the young man. However, she was careful to not to show any sign of anger or agitation. "Yes, I've lost a few pounds, but I won't be holding my breath until that modeling career kicks into high gear." Her words drew a laugh from the boy.

"No, seriously Mrs. Bell, you look great," he insisted, then let his words hang in the air around them. Marion found herself mystified by Jimmy Sullivan's fawning. She had always been immune to male flattery in the past but found herself strangely intrigued by this young man.

"So, have you finally broken down and bought some groceries?"

"I haven't had to. I've been breaking into your house and raiding your fridge every night. Jesus, what's with all the cauliflower?" he clowned. His words were followed by an innocent bump to the hip. Marion was unresponsive for the moment as she tried to rationalize away young Jimmy's behavior. Dumbfounded by his words and actions, she could only conclude that Jimmy Sullivan, the handsome stud twenty-five years her junior, was aggressively flirting with her.

"Jimmy, I could be totally out to lunch, but all of this flattery is coming off as flirtation and we both know nothing's going to happen," she stated. The twenty-two-year old's head dropped in response to her words.

"Hey, Mrs. Bell, I'm really sorry if I insulted or offended you." She reached out and grabbed hold of his wrist.

"Insulted, I am not. Offended? I am anything but offended," she confessed.

"I'd appreciate it if you didn't say anything to Mr. Bell when he gets here. I've had a tough time of it since the whole Melissa nightmare. I guess I better sharpen up on my flirting? I'm a little out of practice." Relieved, Marion playfully returned his hip bump.

"No, it's just the whole age thing. Your flattery skills are just fine," she reassured him.

They walked the quarter of a mile back to the harbor parking lot together. The conversation had turned mundane with opinions on the weather, Route 1 traffic and the coming onslaught of tourists dominating their discussion. All the while Marion found herself becoming increasingly impressed with Jimmy Sullivan. There was a wholesome genuineness about him that she thought lost among his generation. Additionally, there was nary a trace of bitterness in his demeanor, even after what he read as a rejection of his playful flirting. They reached the parking lot and turned onto Atlantic Avenue. Looking up at the twenty-two-year old, she caught him staring at her admiringly.

"If you don't already have dinner plans, you're welcome to join me. I've got to warn you, it will be a meal dominated by lean meat. I'm sure I can manage to get some potatoes on your plate. I've also come up with a dessert of fresh strawberries and my own whipped cream. It's to die for! I can't have them on my diet, but I'll run up to the IGA and get you a package of those angel cake shells." Marion had blurted out the invitation on impulse. The long walk had awakened something fresh and new and perhaps even sexual in her. The Sullivan boy paused momentarily before responding.

"Yeah, that'd be nice," he answered, accepting the invitation.

"Why don't we shoot for seven?" she suggested.

"Seven's good." confirmed Jimmy. The acceptance in place, Marion stared blankly at the pavement in front of her, attempting to rationalize her own actions. Less than a half hour earlier she had rebuffed Jimmy Sullivan's flirtatious advances. Now he was to be her dinner guest at the house that evening. She wondered what kind of signals was she sending out and why was she doing it? It was as if little Marion MacDermott, her fifteen-year-old self, had taken possession of her mind. God knows she would have no wish to take hold of her body. Her imagination was racing uncontrollably while Jimmy made small talk from a foot away. She directed her thoughts back to the conversation at hand. By all appearances, the Sullivan boy had not noticed her temporary disappearance from their discussion.

It was still early afternoon when the two walkers arrived home. Marion slipped into a pair of jeans and drove to the grocery store. She did not want Jimmy suffering any discomfort conforming to her strict, Atkins diet and picked up a few items including rolls and potatoes. By the middle of the afternoon, she was resting on her porch lounger clutching a glass of white wine and wondering if she was putting too much stock into what would probably turn into a very innocent dinner.

Jimmy made the journey of ten steps from his family's porch to the back entrance to Marion's cottage and arrived precisely at seven o'clock. With his appearance at the back door the woman mockingly checked her watch.

"Did you run into any traffic on the way over," she called out through the screen door.

"Some, but I managed to hit every light and avoided making a bad first impression by being late," he answered.

"It's a little late on that whole first impression thing. You lost out on that your first morning here when you had to beg for a cup of coffee." The Sullivan boy stepped inside the door and eased himself onto the nearest comfortable chair. Marion noticed he had cleaned up for the evening. He had donned a pair of unwrinkled Bermuda shorts and a buttoned short-sleeved shirt. His longish auburn hair was combed and visibly damp, no doubt from time spent in the shower. "Let me pour you a glass of wine," she suggested. Her words brought a pained expression to the young man's face.

"I actually bought us wine this afternoon. It's chilling in the fridge back at my house," he confessed. Marion waived him off.

"For next time," she answered, then realized the implication of her words. *Am I out of my mind? What's next, an unsolicited back massage? Get a grip on yourself.* It was at this moment that Marion realized she had spent too much of her afternoon anticipating this casual dinner and far too much time fixating on the physical qualities of Jimmy Sullivan. She retreated to the kitchen and pulled two bottles of white Zinfandel from the refrigerator. She had chosen this specific wine because it was the nearest thing to soda she could come up with and Jimmy's tender years were still a psychological issue with her. During her time in the kitchen she noticed a drop-off in the conversation. The effortless flow of ideas and observations from just the afternoon before was no longer there. She returned to the living room with beverages in hand. Jimmy's eyes were trained on her. After serving her guest, she took a seat in the adjacent chair to him. The room was quiet for the next few moments except for the sound of the lapping waves twenty yards away. Both seemed powerless to address the awkward lull in the conversation. It was Jimmy who made the first attempt to open dialogue.

"On our first date, Melissa and I found ourselves sitting in a coffee shop before a movie with absolutely nothing to say. Then she came up with this thing about sharing something personal with one another. It had to be something we were a little embarrassed about. In other words, we had to show some trust in the other person." Marion took a lengthy sip from her wine glass.

"Are you suggesting that we do something along those lines?" The Sullivan boy nodded his head in the affirmative. Marion giggled and sat back in her chair, lifting her legs up and onto a nearby ottoman. "You first," she insisted behind an amused smile. He swallowed a mouthful of wine and leaned forward.

"Okay, but no mocking the other person after they've come clean, right?" Marion agreed with a nod of her head. "Back when I was thirteen or fourteen I was rummaging through a bunch of my father's stuff out in the garage and came upon a small stack of his vinyl record albums. It wasn't a big pile, and out of curiosity I began sifting through them. It only took a couple of seconds to realize that his pitiful collection was made up of only two groups, the Mamas and the Papas and the Fifth Dimension. Looking down at the album covers, I was quickly struck by a couple of the girls in the groups. Michelle Phillips of the Mamas and Papas and Marilyn McCoo of the Fifth Dimension were so beautiful I couldn't believe my eyes. I had never found women from other time periods attractive before for some reason, maybe because of hair styles or how they made up their faces, but these two just blew me away. Knowing my dad wouldn't miss them, I moved the albums up to my room, so I could just look at these girls. Keep in mind, I was fourteen-years-old, so you can probably imagine how these two girls worked their way into my fantasies," suggested Jimmy. His words bought a round of laughter from Marion. "A couple of days later I found myself alone with my dad. I told him about spotting the albums in the garage and innocently questioned him on the lack of anything but Fifth Dimension and Mamas and Papas albums in his collection. He explained that his collection had once been much larger than it was now but that he had tossed or given away everything else. That's when he admitted to having a crush on a couple of the girls in those two groups and held onto the albums for sentimental reasons, a fact that blew my mind." Jimmy flashed Marion a sheepish smile and took a sip of wine. She responded with a respectful round of applause.

"Bravo. Thank you for that insight into both you and your father's private thoughts. Correct me if I'm wrong but I don't remember either of those women being anything but fully dressed on their album covers," observed Marion. Jimmy rolled his eyes.

"The fourteen-year-old me and my imagination had no problem dealing with that, I assure you," he replied.

"Refill?" she asked, pointing to his empty glass of wine. He indicated yes. "Fifteen more minutes on the chicken," she called out from the kitchen.

Marion returned to the living room with two glasses filled to the brim. Settling back into her chair, she was immediately called upon for her personal anecdote.

"This, too, will be a story from my teenage years back in Connecticut. In the summer between junior high and my freshman year of high school, I had a mad crush on a boy named Danny Flynn. He was a couple of years older than me but lived in the neighborhood, so I saw him quite a bit. During the long summer vacation from school the kids in the neighborhood would often go the pond to swim and cool off. One day my friend, Susan, and I planned to go down to the pond to see if we could get the boys to invite us to join them and splash around a little. Yes, the plan was to maybe flirt our way into their inner circle. For me, it was a chance to get Danny to know I was alive. Well, our plan went out the window when Susan was forced to babysit her much younger sister. Crushed, I came up with an alternate plan and set off for the pond alone. You see, I happened to know where the boys would strip down and leave their clothes before swimming. It was in an area of very thick bushes. So, while the boys were raising hell down in the water, I sneaked into the bushes and grabbed Danny's Red Sox shirt and made off with it. I had brought a large bag with me to conceal it from prying eyes and I took it home with me. I took it home and up to my room. From that day on I had my own piece of Danny Flynn to hold next to me in the privacy of my own room and to breathe in whenever the urge arose." Jimmy broke into a round of applause.

"If those had been girls in the pond, I'm not sure I would have had the strength to settle for a shirt," he blurted out. Marion laughed into her glass. *Are you listening to yourself and him? This sounds like something from a frat party. What the hell are you doing here? You're forty-seven fucking years old!* Marion suddenly felt embarrassed. She fidgeted in her chair. "Oh, I've been meaning to ask you something." She gestured for him to continue. "I feel a little embarrassed calling you Marion. To be honest, it's a very stuffy name. And there's no way I'm going to call you Mrs. Bell." She nodded her understanding.

"In my distant youth, my friends called me Marnie, like from the movie."

"What movie?" She rolled her eyes.

"Ah, there's that generational thing. It's a Hitchcock movie from back in the sixties," she explained.

"Him, I've heard of."

The meal was served on the porch overlooking the ocean. To accommodate Jimmy there were warmed rolls and baked potatoes. Thanks to the sharing of secrets from their teenage years the conversation began to flow effortlessly. She learned that Jimmy would begin work the following Monday with a lawn maintenance company. This pleased her. She was also gratified by his appetite. Cooking had never been her strong suit, but the young man seemed to appreciate his homecooked meal. The sun's rays had just ceased to brighten the waters off Wells Beach when her neighbor's tone turned more serious.

"You never said anything about Mr. Bell when I asked you earlier. When are you expecting him to arrive?" Marion looked down at her plate and took up playing with her remaining food. "I mean…everything with us is quite innocent and we have nothing to hide." Marion locked eyes with her young admirer. In the diminishing light, he appeared even younger than his twenty-two years.

"Monty walked out on me just before Christmas last year. The divorce is already final. That's why I'm up here alone right now. The house came to me in the settlement," she announced. Jimmy reached out and took the last dinner roll from the table while he processed his neighbor's words. He buttered the roll, his mind presumably deep in thought. She responded to the break in the conversation by swallowing the remaining few drops of wine in her glass. She was waiting on a verbal response from her guest when he suddenly pushed his chair back from the table and rose to his feet. She stared up at him, studying his face for a reaction. Stepping around the table he dropped to his knees and stared intently at her face and eyes. "Not so close if you don't mind. I don't need you seeing my laugh lines quite this clearly," she joked. His eyes remained trained on her. He gestured to her to stand and she complied. Pushing her back against a porch window he pressed his lips against hers and pushed her body against the back wall of the porch. She had not seen this act of sexual aggression coming. She welcomed his mouth and lips for a moment before pushing him away. "What was that?" He drew in a deep breath.

"I've been holding myself back since the morning you invited me over for coffee, telling myself your husband would be joining you shortly and we didn't need something like this hanging in the air. Marnie, do you have any idea how incredibly attracted I am to you?" She shook her head and waved him away. The twenty-two-year old made no attempt to step back. Pushing her way by him, she pulled open the screen door and entered the house.

"Oh please, stop it with the Marnie thing. You can't make a silk purse out of a sow's ear. I'm a middle aged, unemployed divorcee, not some twenty-year-old back on campus," she reasoned. He shook his head in disbelief.

"You are a sexy, desirable woman with a great body, a body that seems to get sexier with each passing day and a level of class far beyond anything I've run into at college in the last few years," he argued. *He's trying to prey on your vulnerability. He's horny and you're an arm's length away and pathetic.* Stepping around him, she made her way into the kitchen, quickly reaching the sink where a handful of unwashed dishes waited on her attention. She snatched a sponge from the countertop and nervously began washing the caked food from the surface of the plates. Jimmy Sullivan followed her into the room and stepped to within a few inches of her. Placing his hands on her shoulders, he drew his body closer to her and softly peppered the back of her neck with kisses. The naked aggression on display only seconds earlier was gone. Her body stiffened but did not recoil while she waited on his next move.

"I'm not ready for something like this," she declared. She constructed her words carefully. Her hope was to call an end to the proceedings. However, deep within her, there was the urge to keep the fire burning within her young guest, if not burning then at least smoldering. "If you could give me just a little time to sort out my feelings…" He brought his fingertips up to her mouth, cutting off her sentence. He spun her around and stared into her eyes.

"One kiss. If you would give me one meaningful kiss then, I promise you, I will be perfectly civil the rest of the night," he stated in a near whisper. She felt his warm breath on her face.

"One kiss," she answered, extending her index finger. Without hesitation, Jimmy cupped her face within the palms of his hands and brought his lips in contact with her own. Wedged between the sink and her twenty-two-year old neighbor, she let her body loosen up. The pressure brought against her body was not excessive and she felt the early stages of arousal. The Sullivan boy made no attempt to force his tongue between her lips, content to press and release his lips on the edges of her mouth. The sacrificial kiss went on, Marion becoming more and more aware of his body pressed against her own. He was aroused, she thought. Taking the initiative, she plunged her tongue between his lips. He returned the gesture causing the embrace to tighten. She felt her body temperature rise. The kiss continued for a few moments more.

"Jimmy, that's enough," she insisted, pushing his body back to arm's length. "You're very attractive and I've grown quite fond of you over the last week, but I think we should call the evening to an end," she insisted. There was no uncertainty in her tone. He took in a lung full of oxygen and nodded his head in agreement. Ushering her guest to the door, Marion made a point of placing her hand on his shoulder while stepping from the house, a gesture intended to relay her openness to their budding relationship.

On this night, Marion had difficulty dropping off to sleep, her mind reliving the events at the house only hours earlier. *Okay, I seem to have a possible cheap thrill for the asking. The kid seems to have no problem with the issue of age or wrinkles for that matter. He really seems like a nice boy. What I don't need is to become fond of the young man and then have to suffer through the end of the relationship. He's not going to remain available long. It isn't even Memorial Day yet. Once the days grow warm the beach will be teeming with teenyboppers and college girls. All the hair dye in the world isn't going to be able to compete with that. And then there's the matter of Jerry and May Sullivan. I can't even imagine looking them in the eye after they've learned their baby boy has been sharing my bed and the cougar from hell has had her way with him.* Marion burst into a fit of laughter at the thought of her name being branded with the cougar label. She rolled herself out of bed, making her way to the second-floor bathroom and turned on the light. She stared into the oval mirror above the sink. *You are an attractive woman and there is no way you look forty-seven.* She pursed her lips and gazed at her image, trying to pretend she was seeing herself for the first time. *You can easily pass for thirty-eight or thirty-nine. My God, you have this handsome kid just out of college fawning all over you. You must look pretty damn good for your age. Do the math. There may be a twenty-five-year age gap but if you look eight or nine years younger than you are, isn't it really more like fifteen? I remember reading somewhere that there were four ways measuring age. There was how old you looked, how old you felt, how old you acted and how old you were in years. The point being made was that chronological age was the least important. Besides, there is barely a wrinkle on your face. You've always had that oily skin of yours. Now, it's clear, it was a blessing in disguise.* With the pep talk over, she clicked off the light and returned to her bed.

Chapter 3

In the week and a half following their dinner and kiss, Marion and Jimmy saw little of each other. On the weekend following their evening together Jimmy attended a baseball team reunion back in Connecticut. During this time, Marion stuck fast to her Atkin's Diet and daily walks along the beach. On the Saturday of Memorial Day weekend, Marion tossed off her bedsheets and faithfully made the walk to the bathroom and her scale. She was currently in a slump with her weight seemingly stuck on one hundred and thirty-seven pounds. Placing her bare feet on the surface of the scale, she stared down and waited for the black indicator to settle on a number. The mechanism shifted back and forth before finally resting on one hundred, thirty-four and one-half pounds. Raising her face toward the heavens, she let out with a triumphant scream of delight.

"Sweet Jesus, I've done it," she called out to the empty house. "That's over eleven pounds in under two weeks." She scampered downstairs and rushed to the kitchen, turning on the coffee maker. If Maureen were alive she would have already dialed her up. She needed to share her news with someone. Entering the living room, she grabbed the remote and turned on Fox and Friends. The television popped on within seconds. Marion thought of calling Mia but was afraid of getting her ex-husband's young paramour. Just the thought of that brought on a mild urge to vomit. She walked out onto the porch and stared over at the Sullivan house. Jimmy's car was parked out by the road along with two others. He had company, she thought. Although anxious to share her diet news with him she decided to put off interrupting his morning until nine o'clock or until she was sure he was up. Ducking back inside the house, she poured a cup of coffee and ascended the stairs in search of a summer outfit befitting her new figure. Following ten minutes of scouring her closet, she decided on a white, two-piece outfit that would do justice to her toned body. After laying the outfit out on the bed, she went in search of a pair of white sandals.

It was sometime after eight-thirty when Marion emerged from her shower and slipped into her halter top and form-fitting shorts. She was admiring herself in the bedroom mirror when she heard activity from over at the Sullivan house. The activity included Jimmy's voice. Taking a final look at herself in the mirror, she exited her bedroom and walked downstairs to her back porch. The sun was already warming the air along the shoreline when she scampered down the two steps to her sandy backyard and made the short walk to the Sullivan house. Scurrying onto her neighbor's porch, she peeked in through the window and knocked. Out of sight there came a rush of activity before Jimmy materialized from inside of the house. He flashed her a nervous smile and made his way to the door.

"I was hoping to speak to you last night, but we came in too late," he explained while joining her on the porch. "I have company," he muttered while stepping outside. Marion answered with an abbreviated burst of laughter.

"No big deal," she responded and glanced over his shoulder.

"Jim...your pots and pans, where do your parent's keep them?" called out a female voice from a couple of rooms away. Marion's glance turned in the direction of the voice and then back to Jimmy. He appeared unnerved. She looked back into the house and watched as a male and two females emerged from the far room.

"Again, I hoped to speak with you last night, but we came in too late. This is nothing like it appears." One of the young women walked into the adjoining room, leaning her cheek seductively against the door jamb. She was scantily clothed and gave the appearance of having just rolled out of bed.

"Jimbo? Pots and pans?" asked the girl. She was blond, curvaceous and smelled of sex from six feet away.

"Under the counter, Juliet. All the way to the right and under the counter," instructed Jimmy. The girl shot Marion a condescending glance and went in search of the kitchenware. Jimmy turned back to his neighbor.

"I just came over to...damn it, I can't even remember why I came over," Marion confessed and pushed her way past Jimmy. He reached out and grabbed her by the wrist. "Take your goddamn hands off me," she spat out and sprinted toward her house.

"What the fuck is her problem?" called out the girl from the house.

"Cool it, Juliet. Just cool it," called back Jimmy to the girl.

Marion entered the house and locked the door behind her. Seconds later she was bounding up the stairs to the sound of knocking at her back door. Reaching her bedroom, she grabbed for the television remote. Seconds later the room was filled with the voice of a news commentator. She turned up the volume to drown out the sound of knocking from downstairs. Pulling a pillow out from under the bed covers, she leaned back against the headboard and stared thoughtlessly at the television. *What the hell was I thinking? Did you really think that, at age forty-seven, you could hold the attention of a young stud for more than a day and a half? For God's sake, Marion, wake up and act your age. You're so far past your prime it isn't even funny. Now, thanks to your delusional fantasy, you've humiliated yourself publicly. Those four, Generation X pups over there must be having quite a laugh at your expense right about now. All your daydreaming about a roll in the hay with a boy less than half your age has come to a screeching halt. He's landed a young lollipop for his bed and the thought of dragging your tired carcass up to his bedroom must seem like a nightmare averted right about now.* She stared past the television and out the window. Her eyes were filling with tears. It dawned on her that it was only Saturday. She would have an entire three-day weekend to suffer through. She knew she could not face Jimmy

Sullivan. She would have to avoid any face-to-face encounter. The kitchen was well stocked with food and drink. She would get through it, she thought.

Marion opened her eyes following a period of deep sleep. Glancing at the alarm clock, she saw it was a few minutes past eleven-thirty. Her depression and a brief crying fit had led to a couple of hours of escape. The television was still on. She plucked the remote from her night stand and turned it off. For a moment, she thought her encounter with Jimmy at the Sullivan house had been something out of a nightmare. A fraction of a second later she realized it was not. She lay motionless in bed, fully dressed, for another minute before the sound of young voices drifted up from the beach. Her curiosity aroused, she rose from the bed and made her way to the bedroom window. On the sand below a net was erected a few feet down the beach and four young people were sided up for a game of volleyball. Straining her eyes, she could make out Jimmy and a young girl on the far side of the net. Nearer to her was a muscular male teamed up with the girl she had encountered a few hours earlier. She stared down on the young people from the shadows of her bedroom knowing she could do so undetected. The two girls were garbed in the skimpiest of bathing suits. By all appearances the girl who smelled of sex earlier that morning was the older of the two, young women. Both females were very pretty. She watched until the sight of Jimmy outside in the company of his friends became painful. Sensing an opportunity to leave the house undetected, Marion hurriedly changed into jeans and a sweatshirt and drove the Toyota onto Atlantic Avenue and away from the house.

The afternoon was spent in Portsmouth where Marion took in a matinee movie and browsed the trendy, downtown shops of the city. In the waning minutes of the afternoon she felt a wave of loneliness sweep over her. Driving northward on Route 1, she played with the idea of calling her daughter. Mia had made the choice of living with her father and there had been preciously little communication with her since that decision but there had never been an argument or conflict preventing her from trying to call her daughter. In the end, Marion decided to forego the call down to Connecticut and opted for a walk at Long Sands in York before returning to Wells Beach. She arrived home to a darkened house and quickly made her way inside. The Sullivan residence was also blanketed in darkness. Marion hastily made her way into the house, grabbed a couple of cans of soda and a bag of munchies, and made her way upstairs for the night. She needed to be far from the front and back doors in the event Jimmy came over. She wanted no eye contact with him and was in no mood to hear any lame excuses involving his weekend guests. What she needed was nothing more than to put the notion of a personal relationship between the two to an early grave. It was shortly after ten o'clock when she clicked off the light and settled in for a night's sleep. Outside her oceanfront windows the wind had picked up, sending her Boothbay Harbor chimes into a symphony of wild, melodic notes.

Chapter 4

For Marion Bell, the Memorial Day weekend of 2002 dragged on like a mid-summer root canal procedure carried out in a dingy building lacking both air conditioning or proper ventilation. On Sunday morning, a lethargic Marion slept in until nearly twelve o'clock. Trapped in her own house for fear of running into Jimmy in the yard, her day was cursed mostly by the voices of the two young women and one muscular young man holed up next door. Largely absent from the chorus of youthful voices was that of Jimmy's. By Sunday evening she felt like a prisoner in her own house. It was then that she decided to go out for dinner on Memorial Day. She decided to make the short drive up Mile Road to Billy's Chowder House. It was a restaurant frequented by tourists and locals alike and had a bar where, under the right conditions and with a little luck, she could strike up an acquaintance with a gentleman close to her age. Lastly, she would venture out on the last night of the holiday weekend at a time when so many of the out-of-state people would already be on the road.

By five-thirty in the afternoon, Marion was primed for her night out of the house. Jimmy and his houseguests had driven off in all three cars two hours earlier. Dressed in a pair of designer jeans and a pink blouse, she was more than satisfied with her appearance for her simple night out. Since her separation and divorce from Monty, she had mostly avoided all appearances in the general public where she would be viewed as a single. For this reason, this evening away from the house constituted a major step forward in her life as a divorced and available woman. Turning onto Mile Road, she thought back to the previous summer when she and Maureen hung out at Billy's Chowder House and, to an extent, held court over other patrons their age. What an incredible difference a year makes, she thought. Pulling into the parking lot, she was pleased to find an empty space on the side of building. She inhaled a deep breath of ocean air and emerged from the car. She was nervous but took consolation in the knowledge that this was Billy's Chowder House, a family restaurant frequented by upper middle-class patrons. She was also buoyed by her appearance this evening, a pink, printed blouse tucked into designer jeans that hugged her now well contoured legs.

Marion was greeted at the door and informed there were a few open stools in the lounge. Making her way along the combination hallway and waiting area, she entered the lounge and looked up and down the rectangular bar. *Ah, the good news is there are a couple of empty seats over by the far window. The bad news is most everyone already seated seems to be in couples.* She walked the full length of the room and claimed a stool beside a woman approximately her age. The woman, casually dressed and sporting a mane of reddish hair, was in the company of a man with a sunburned face and drooping moustache. Settling in atop her stool, she scanned the length of the bar and examined the faces assembled. Most people were engaged in conversation and appeared unaware of her arrival. A few seconds passed before the bartender, Amy, introduced herself and offered to take Marion's order. *Oh great, the bartender's tall, thin, young and attractive, just what I needed tonight. The weekend from hell rolls on without missing a beat.* Marion ordered a dry martini but waived off a dinner menu for the moment.

"Even if you don't order dinner, you have to have a bowl of chowder. Their chowder is to die for," remarked the woman with the bushy, red hair seated next to her. She turned and extended the woman a courteous smile.

"I've been coming here for quite a few years, so you don't have to convince me," she answered. Turning toward the woman, Marion tried to engage her in conversation but found the woman's attention was already being reclaimed by her husband. *Wow, this whole single thing is rough. I was spoiled for twenty years with Monty always there. I know this is at least partly psychological. How many business trips did I go on over the years and never felt anything like this?* She let out a silent sigh of relief when her martini arrived. It provided her with something to fiddle with and fixate her eyes upon. The next ten minutes of her time was spent in silence. The couple seated on her immediate left were already through their desserts and waiting on their tabs. Around her, Marion observed the activity at the restaurant picking up. Older couples and families seated at tables overlooking the harbor were gradually being replaced by a younger crowd of customers. A roar of laughter rose from the far side of the bar and she lifted her eyes from the martini. She established momentary eye contact with a handful of people and exchanged smiles. Her eyes drifted down to her watch. *Jesus, you've been sitting here for nearly twenty minutes. Put an end to your suffering and pay your bill.* The bartender's attention was currently taken up filling an order for a table of eight. *I'll wait until the poor girl's done with this order before I ask for my tab.* The couple seated next to her rose from their stools and began their walk to the door, leaving Marion with two empty seats to her left and a single, empty seat on her right. Scanning the far side of the bar she locked eyes with a pair of women and exchanged smiles. *The people are so nice here and I can tell they feel uncomfortable for me. Oh God, help me get the bartender's attention.* Marion focused her eyes on the far dining room. A head of bushy, auburn hair had grabbed her attention. *Oh, for the love of God, not him.* She had caught sight of Jimmy Sullivan making his way to a table in the company of his three houseguests. Behind her, a couple hovered over the empty seats on her left but then decided to join friends at a nearby window table. Her social isolation lingered on. Finally, the bartender concluded her transaction with the party of eight and turned in her direction. Marion lifted a hand and caught the young woman's attention. Amy gestured back to her, indicating she had made note of her request. Marion's eyes dropped down to her martini. The glass was only a few sips from full. Her fingers fumbled through her handbag in search of cash.

"I hope you're not about to leave?" A pair of hands came down onto Marion's shoulders, startling her. "What a stroke of freaking luck running into you here," exclaimed Jimmy Sullivan while sliding his body between Marion and the nearest stool. Temporarily speechless, she peered deep into the twenty-two-year old's eyes in search of sarcasm. None was visible.

"Shouldn't you be back in the next room? It's hardly a romantic foursome without you." Jimmy pulled back in astonishment and scanned her face for additional meaning behind her words. He shot her an expression of disbelief.

"Oh, there's plenty of passion and romance over there in the next room but none of it belongs to me," he explained calmly. She rolled her eyes in a display of skepticism and turned her attention back to the surface of the bar and her martini.

"Hey, I really missed coming over to the house this weekend, but I had an obligation to attend to."

"Oh please, spare me. I'm not some emptyheaded college girl who will swallow any hairbrained story you can throw at me." Jimmy shook his head in frustration and claimed the stool beside his beachfront neighbor.

"Just hear me out," he insisted calmly. Now it was Marion searching her young friend's face for any trace of sincerity. She beckoned him to proceed with his explanation after only a moment's hesitation. Duane McKinley is an acquaintance from college. I can't say he was a friend. We never hung out in the same crowd. Anyway, it had to be a couple of months ago, we found ourselves out crawling bars together along with another half dozen or so guys. It was down in Hartford and the whole gang of us wandered into the wrong bar. I must have been really pissed out of my mind because I apparently started running my mouth off. There were mostly blacks in the bar and there was this one table of what seemed like bad dudes. Again, I was really drunk and God knows what crap was coming out of my mouth. Well, I probably had a good kick in the ass coming but a couple of these guys proceeded to really start beating the shit out of me. My so-called buddies all made for the door to save their own asses, all except Duane. He came back and truly saved my ass. If you saw him at all this weekend you know he's a powerfully built guy and he can handle himself in a fight. He risked his ass by coming back, gave at least as well as he took, and managed to drag me back to the car pretty much in one piece. He took a few blows to the head and body for me. I owed him something and told him so the next day." Marion mockingly raised her eyes to the ceiling.

"If you're about to tell me that you shacked up with one of those girls to repay a debt to this Duane character then spare me," she scoffed. Jimmy raised a finger to her lips.

"I'm not done. Please hear me out. Duane called me the middle of last week and asked if I was ready to pay him back for, if not saving my life, then at least saving my front teeth. After learning it was nothing dangerous or illegal, I consented. I've got to be honest here, I'm a little afraid of Duane. He's not the kind of guy you say no to, particularly when you're indebted to him. When he called he explained that he had met a girl that he really liked and had a chance to spend a long weekend with her. Duane knew I had my parent's house in Wells for the summer and remembered how I had promised him some time there in appreciation for saving my ass in Hartford." Marion rolled her eyes and swigged down the rest of her drink. She was not buying Jimmy's explanation. He took hold of her wrist. "Please Marion, hear me out. Duane went on to explain that his payback was to come in two parts. First, a long Memorial Day weekend at my folk's house and second, I was to entertain Juliet's sister, her sixteen-year-old sister, Danielle, over the weekend. Apparently, Juliet, who is all of nineteen, couldn't get permission from her folks to take off from home without a chaperone. So, not only was I left hopelessly longing to spend time with you and you being no more than thirty feet away in the next house but also tied down to a teenybopper who, if I gave into my mild temptation, might earn me eight to twenty years behind bars. It was the weekend from hell," he declared sheepishly. Marion stared across the room while processing the details of her friend's explanation. "I wanted to let you know what was going on all weekend but whenever I came over to the house you wouldn't answer the door." Following a few moments of hesitation, she turned her head in his direction.

"Your excuse is so idiotic, so incredibly stupid, it almost assuredly has to be true. James, you are forgiven. Why don't we reset everything back to where they were on day one," she declared just as the bartender finally approached with her tab. He took hold of her hand.

"Hey Marion, don't leave," he implored. "I haven't had dinner yet and I don't want to sit here alone. Please join me, my treat." Amy, the bartender, stood frozen in front of her, bar tab in hand, and waited on Marion's response to Jimmy Sullivan's invitation. Marion, plastic already in hand, hesitated for a moment before locking eyes with her young admirer. Her mind flashed back to their heartfelt kiss in her kitchen. *If this were any other twenty-two-year old male on the planet you know what your answer would be.* She hesitated before glancing up to the bartender. Amy's eyes twinkled and shot her the faintest of smiles.

"Okay, what the hell?" she answered.

"I'll bring you two over a menu," responded the bartender before turning away.

The evening meal and conversation exceeded Marion's expectations. She talked at length about her friendship with Maureen Brady and how difficult it had been becoming reconciled to the fact that she no longer had her friend to confide in or with whom to share good or painful news. She asked Jimmy if he had come upon such a friend in his short life and he had indicated that he had not. Over the course of the ninety-minute meal, Marion had, more than once, noticed others seated at the bar taking in the sight of a middle-aged woman in the company of a much younger man. *What must be going on in their minds? Their first thought must be that Jimmy is the good son, taking out his mother for the evening to celebrate some major anniversary in his father's absence. That, of course, is until they pick up on the subtle way he makes contact, resting his hand on my shoulder or brushing a few stray hairs back from over my eye. No, these are not the actions of the devoted son unless his name is Oedipus.*

With their plates and glasses empty and having passed on another round of drinks, the pair watched the bartender hesitate momentarily before placing their bill on the counter in front of Jimmy. Reaching for the tab, he was stopped short by Marion who insisted on financing their evening.

"No, this is a guy thing," he insisted while plucking the statement from her.

"Come on now. The truth of the matter is I can pretty much buy and sell you at this point in our respective lives. There's nothing to be ashamed of. I've had a wonderful evening thanks to you. You saved me from leaving Billy's with my tail between my legs," she assured him.

"Please, people are watching us, and I'd rather not look like a schmuck," he argued. "If it takes a week or so to financially recover from this night then so be it. In truth, it was worth it," he declared. Marion turned to him and stared penetratingly into his eyes, holding her attention on him for a few seconds. Tilting her head slightly she brought her lips up to his ear.

"What if we compromise? Why don't you pay for our meals and I'll reimburse you for my share outside?" He smiled and nodded approvingly.

"I can live with that," he answered before reaching into his back pocket. "Oh, I will have to bum a ride home from you. I'm sure Duane and the girls are long gone by now." She shot Jimmy an obliging nod and sipped down the last of her beverage. She rose to her feet and took stock of her herself. She felt the effect of a mild buzz but nothing enough to question her ability to drive the approximately one mile back to the house. She walked the length of the bar and looked back toward Jimmy who was settling the bill with the bartender and counting out a gratuity. She was conscious of more than one pair of male eyes trained on her. She felt attractive and pleased she had made the decision to venture from the house on this night. She waited by the doorway leading back into the hall until Jimmy joined her. He held up a single finger and gestured toward the men's room door. Marion stepped to the side of the hall and waited on her young companion. Glancing downward, she made eye contact with a familiar face. Betsy Chase had waited on Monty and her over the last few years and become acquainted with the former couple. The trim waitress shot her a knowing smile.

"Three or four of us girls would like to know your secret," she joked. "You haven't made a pact with the devil, have you?" Marion laughed heartily before bringing her hand up to her mouth. She nodded in the negative.

"Just the opposite. It's been a pretty rough year and God's decided to throw me a bone," replied a delighted Marion. A moment later the men's room door swung open and Jimmy appeared. Stepping across the hallway, he reached his arm around her shoulder and guided her toward the front door. *He's treating me like his date. Doesn't he feel even a little foolish. I mean, his hand is draped over my shoulder and he's got to see some of the looks he's getting from the people around us.*

Jimmy Sullivan made no attempt to claim the driver's seat. Standing by the front, passenger door, he waited patiently until Marion released the lock. Within seconds, he was seated beside her, seat belts fastened. He turned his body in her direction.

"Thank you for an evening of intelligent, adult conversation," he stated. "You're not too hard on the eyes either and that combination makes for a delightful night. I'm glad we cleared up that whole matter about Duane and the girls. If it's okay with you, we can settle the whole reimbursement thing back at the house." She agreed to his suggestion and they pulled away from Billy's Chowder House, motoring due east toward the Atlantic Ocean. Turning left onto Atlantic Avenue, she could feel the focus of his eyes on her. "Oh, and if you wouldn't mind I hoped to ask you a question about last Saturday." She shot him a slightly irritated glance.

"Join me in the house. Then you can ask me your question and I'll consider answering it."

Chapter 5

Glasses of wine were poured before Jimmy found himself following Marion into the living room. She was careful to select a chair in the corner of the room and not the couch where he could possibly slide in next to her. It was he who claimed a spot on the couch and made himself comfortable. Marion slipped off her shoes and propped her feet atop the chair's matching ottoman.

"Okay, I'm ready," she indicated while staring across the room. He smiled back.

"First, before any question, I want to go on record in saying you look great tonight. Your weight loss to absolute perfection is clearly accomplished. I must have spent ninety percent of the drive back to the house just staring down at your long legs and tight jeans," he confessed. The words out, his face broke into a sheepish smile.

"Thank you. A girl can't get nearly enough of that kind of feedback, particularly after having had her ego battered around for the past twelve months." *My God, I can't believe how fine he looks tonight and I don't think that's just the alcohol working on me.* Marion broke eye contact with her young admirer and stared up at the ceiling before closing her eyes. "Enough flattery. End the suspense. What is this burning question you needed to ask me, Mr. Sullivan?" She heard him muffle a giggle.

"Okay, well, Mr. Sullivan would love to know exactly why you came over to the house on Saturday morning. I couldn't help but notice that you were dressed to kill and that struck me odd at the time given it was only nine o'clock in the morning." Marion reacted with a wry smile.

"If you must know, I had just weighed in and learned that I had reached, no, surpassed my goal of one hundred and thirty-five pounds. I was feeling really good about myself and wanted to share the moment with a friend." Wanting to appear blasé, Marion's eyes remained closed, her head tilted back.

"And you put that fine outfit on just to share good news with me?"

"Okay, perhaps I was showing off just a little bit. I wasn't just at my ideal weight, I was under it. Perhaps it was just a little, 'if you've got it, flaunt it,' action. A woman is entitled to show off every now and then, isn't she?" Her question went unanswered for a few seconds before she got a response.

"I suppose she is," he answered from what sounded like inches away. She opened her eyes and saw that Jimmy had quietly crossed the room and was now seated on the floor beside the ottoman, his eyes riveted on her. A wave of excitement washed over her. *This is beginning to move beyond the playful banter stage to somewhere more serious. Are you really prepared to plunge into something this unconventional and risqué?* She reached down and played with a few strands of his hair. She felt herself growing wet from excitement. Marion drew in a deep breath. Lacking the strength to encourage him nor the desire to send him away, she rested her head back on the chair and allowed events to simply unfold. "I know you have to be really tired of hearing this, but you look so magnificently hot in these jeans," said Jimmy, following his words with a kiss to one then the other of her thighs. She felt her breathing become more exaggerated. He slipped off her shoes and pushed the ottoman aside. Within seconds it was he propping up the lower half of her body.

"Please think about what you are doing," she cautioned. "I am so not suited for you." Her words lacked even a trace of conviction.

"I have thought about nothing else but this moment since the second I first saw you standing on your porch a few weeks ago looking out to sea." Marion re-opened her eyes and observed Jimmy kneeling on the floor in front of her. "May I be totally honest with you?"

"I expect nothing less," she replied.

"From the time I reached puberty, I remember seeing you up here in the summer and always thinking what a beautiful woman you were. A couple of years back you gained some weight and my infatuation sort of tailed off but by last year you were more yourself again and my infatuation was back."

"I was already having issues with my ex-husband last summer and stress will lead to weight loss, at least it does for me," she declared.

"When I saw you standing out on your porch and sipping on your coffee the whole infatuation thing just came rushing back. Then, after you told me about the divorce, it was like the infatuation turned into an obsession," he confessed. His words were followed by two gentle kisses applied to the inside of her thighs just above her knees. He followed with a second pair of kisses higher on her legs. She reached down and clutched his head between her hands. Her breathing grew even more intense.

"Jimmy, tell me what you want," she instructed.

"Well, to peel off your jeans for starters," he answered. She smiled down on him before closing her eyes and resting her head on the back of the chair. Marion relaxed her body while Jimmy loosened and then slid her denims down her body. Within seconds they were resting in a pile on the floor. *Oh my God, it's been years since Monty tasted me. Jimmy is so young. Can he really be this considerate a lover?* Seconds passed, and Marion wondered if her lover was struggling with second thoughts. It was then she felt the advance of kisses parading up the inside of her leg and ending with the feel of his tongue on the corner of her panties. Her arousal grew, causing Marion to wrap her fingers through his hair and pull. He responded by showering her vaginal area with kisses.

"Take them off," she commanded. Following her instructions, he pulled the delicate undergarment off and tossed it aside. Within moments his tongue was probing and exploring the inner sanctum of her body, sending her into a fit of ecstasy. At this moment she did not care about the age differential between her and her lover. She did not care that she was the recipient of all the sexual pleasure experienced within the four walls of the room while her young lover knelt before her. She did not care that there would be hell to pay if word of this encounter somehow got back to his parents. She did not care about any disapproving looks she might get from jealous women on the street when seen in the company of her young lover. She did not care about the car crash of a conclusion this affair was, no doubt, destined to face in the foreseeable future. Hell, she did not even care that the window shades were up, leaving the two lovers in plain sight of anyone walking Wells Beach under the moonlight. Marion, at this moment in time, only cared about the divine pleasure radiating through her body.

Following fifteen glorious minutes of sexual stimulation, she cupped Jimmy's head in her hands and tilted it upward. Their eyes met.

"I want to go upstairs with you to my bed," she said softly. He smiled, pressed his mouth to her vaginal lips a final time, and slowly rose to his feet. "Put out the lights and then bring me up. I'm afraid we may have put on quite the show for anyone walking the beach tonight," she added. Crossing the room, Jimmy flicked off the lights before returning to her. Pulling her to her feet, he reached down and lifted her into his arms. He walked to the stairwell and started the ascent. Halfway to the second floor, he paused and kissed her with unusual intensity. *I am sure this is like nothing I have ever experienced before. I am so lightheaded I'm not sure I could stand up right now if I had to. His tongue probes the inside of my mouth and I can literally taste my own body on his lips. I know I should have reciprocated with oral sex but I want his penis inside of me right now.*

Reaching her second story bedroom, Jimmy made his way to the bed and carefully lay Marion down. She looked up to her lover and reached out her arms. He raised a single finger and proceeded to remove his clothes. She watched as the removal of each item of clothing provided a better view of his young, trim body. Finally, he stood over her naked. He was aroused even after spending the better part of the last half hour kneeling at her feet and tending to her. He lay down beside her and rode his fingertips over the curves of her torso. *I love the tenderness but not at this moment.* She reached up and snatched her lover by the hair.

"I want you in me," she insisted, pulling him forward and covering his mouth with hers. He complied and within seconds their bodies were one. Marion arched her back and felt Jimmy grow harder within her. The pleasure was already consuming her. She called out to him. "Don't stop, don't ever stop," she commanded. Her mouth moved from his and she found herself biting down on the side of his neck. His flesh tasted of perspiration. She was conscious of flesh between her teeth and she brought pressure down on it. He moaned but continued controlling her body. He moaned a second time.

"Pleasure or pain, Jimmy? Pleasure or pain?"

"Both," he answered. She was nearing orgasm. Her time being serviced in the downstairs chair had proven time well spent. She returned her mouth to his and again tasted the residue of her own sexuality. Then, like a wave breaking on the shore below the bedroom window, the mounting ecstasy within her body broke over her and her torso resonated with pleasure. It took only seconds for Jimmy to match her satisfaction as he cried out before rolling onto the mattress beside her.

"Thank you, Marnie. Thank you so very much," he muttered. Marion exploded into a fit of laughter.

"Marnie? Where did that come from? You haven't called me Marnie since the night I told you about my childhood nickname," she gushed.

"I don't know. It just came to me out of nowhere." She rolled sideways and planted a peck on his cheek. He reciprocated and the two were eye to eye in bed. Marion reached toward her nightstand and snapped on the table light. He stared deeply into her eyes. "Are you up for a compliment?" Jimmy asked.

"Always," she answered.

"You really, I mean really, taste good," he confessed. She gave him a curious look and scanned the room with her eyes.

"I must admit, I have no idea how to respond to that statement. What am I supposed to say? Oh, I bet you say that to all the girls you kneel down in front of," she wisecracked. Jimmy smiled and folded his hands behind the back of his head. "You know, I could actually taste myself on your lips," she declared.

"Then you know how good you taste, right?" She laughed and buried her face in his chest. He lifted Marion's chin and kissed her squarely on the mouth. "I can't believe how intimate and personal we can speak to each other. I could never talk like this to Melissa. She would have just freaked out," he confessed.

"All I know is that this night has done wonders for my ego and self-worth. I know it must sound like I'm beating a dead horse here but the last year has taken a real toll on me," she admitted.

"Hey, we've both taken it on the chin in recent months." She covered his mouth with her hand.

"No more talk about bad things. Tell me more about those summers a few years ago when you had the hots for me," she ordered. He laughed. "Do teenage boys actually develop crushes on older women like that or are you just some kind of weirdo?"

"I think saying I had the hots for you may be a little bit of an exaggeration, but I did catch myself staring at you quite a bit. I distinctly remember this time when you were sitting up on your porch and wearing an orange bikini. You were sitting in one of your wicker chairs but had your legs propped up with your feet resting on the porch railing. I couldn't believe it. Your husband was just talking and walking back and forth like it was nothing while I was climbing the walls over there, binoculars in hand." Marion closed her eyes and radiated a smile.

"Little did I know," she murmured softly. "You know, I think I still have that bikini," she added.

"If you do then you must wear it for me," he answered excitedly. "No, I mean it."

"It would have to be a private showing. There is no way I am going to go parading up and down Wells Beach in that thing," she declared.

"A private showing is fine." Jimmy fell silent, sliding his arm behind her neck and shoulders until his hand was resting on her right breast. They both seemed deep in thought. "You know, I still can't believe I'm lying beside Mrs. Marion Bell right now and that we just made love here at the beach," he admitted. There was no response from Marion. She was deep in thought, wrestling with her new reality.

Chapter 6

Marion lay in bed, alone, more than a week after her long night of carnal pleasure with Jimmy Sullivan. Since the Memorial Day weekend, they had been intimate three times, shared an evening meal six times and attended one film together. On this night she was stressing over her current romantic situation and the potential train wreck that awaited her at the end of the line. In her forty-seven years she had never been in any relationship of the heart that did not have at least one possible, happy ending scenario until now. What made her circumstances particularly sobering was the knowledge that, not under any conditions, could she see herself escape unscathed. However, she was not ready to surrender her young lover to any other woman. This she knew. Also, there was also the consolation of Jimmy himself. He was a kind and considerate young man. When the time came for their affair to crash and burn, she was sure he would make the effort to spare her feelings to the greatest extent possible.

It was Thursday in the second week of June. Marion had planned a long weekend for her and Jimmy up in Bar Harbor. She put this plan in motion after learning that he had never set foot anywhere north of Camden in the state of Maine. She reasoned that no native New Englander should ever reach adulthood without visiting Bar Harbor and Acadia National Park. The hastily put together plan called for them to leave Wells in the late afternoon on Friday and return home late Monday night. Close by the front door, her luggage sat packed and waiting to be loaded into the Toyota. It was late morning and Marion was wrestling with the temptation of paying Congdon's Doughnuts a visit up on Route 1. She had weighed in at one hundred and thirty-three pounds this morning, two pounds under her ideal weight. *Come on Marion ol' girl, you're playing with the house's money. You have two pounds in the bank here. The sugar crullers are as light as a feather. What's the harm?* She had just snatched up her car keys when the kitchen phone rang. Momentarily saved by the bell, she scampered into the kitchen to answer it.

"Hello."

"Hi mom, it's me, Mia. It's been a while and I thought I'd touch base and make sure everything was okay," said her daughter. "School is over till September and things are not as hectic back here at home. How are things up in Maine?"

"Oh, fine dear. I hope things are going well for you and your father." The phone call from her only child had caught her off guard. Her first instinct was to put distance between herself and the daughter who had so disappointed her earlier in the year. "Have you found a job for the summer yet?"

"No, not really. I got a late start and every job that's worth anything has already been taken," reported the nineteen-year-old.

"Come on now, you're a smart girl. I'm sure if you try hard enough, you should be able to apply yourself and find something. What about your father's contacts? I'm sure your dad would be willing to help you out?" There was no response from Mia for a few seconds.

"I was thinking...it might be nice to spend the summer with you up in Maine," she muttered tentatively. "I mean, it's been nearly six months since I saw you. Talking on the phone is not the same." Marion felt a harsh response build inside of her, but the motherly instinct fought back the temptation to unleash it.

"It didn't have to be that way. To be honest, I was really hurt when your spring vacation came and went without so much as a phone call," she reminded her.

"I know, I know, totally my fault. I got caught up with friends and I really felt like I needed some time away from the cold," she explained. "So...would it be okay to come up and stay with you until college reopens?"

"My dearest, I would have no problem putting you up for a week or so but the whole summer would be a problem. I'm just getting accustomed to my new life here in Wells and trying to acclimate. As I said, why not come up for a week or a week and a half? Your old mother has been through a lot in the last year. Baby steps." Marion was attempting to be as diplomatic as possible but, at the same time, make it perfectly clear a summer long stay was out of the question.

"Okay," conceded her daughter, making no attempt to mask her disappointment. "I should be able to make it up by the weekend. How does Saturday afternoon sound?"

"It sounds too early," answered Marion, unwilling to jeopardize her Bar Harbor weekend with Jimmy. "Why not shoot for mid next week. That way you can avoid the Saturday onslaught of tourist arrivals. It may still be off-season but they're already coming." Mia agreed reluctantly. For the next ten minutes Marion peppered her daughter with questions relating to school, health and boys, never bringing up her ex-husband or his new sex partner in residence.

Marion and Jimmy's weekend away came off without a hitch. Arriving at their log cabin, they lit the fireplace and stayed up until the wee hours of the morning. Marion had made it clear up front that she would be financing ninety percent of the romantic getaway and she was true to her word. There was no economizing on restaurants as the two lunched, wined and dined in the most upscale of establishments. Saturday proved to be mostly overcast with showers off and on so Marion spent the day guiding them through upscale gift and antique shops. With the passing of each day, she found herself not just growing more comfortable in the company of Jimmy Sullivan but also becoming increasing fond of him. On Saturday night she did not hesitate to lie naked in front of the fire at his request. Through their time together she remained alert for any sign that his interest in her was on the wane. To date she had observed no evidence of this. On Sunday the two lovers spent most of the day hiking the trails that crisscrossed the face of Acadia National Park. It was early in the afternoon and somewhere far from civilization on Connors Nubble Trail when she abruptly stopped and approached Jimmy on an outcropping of sheer rock.

"Are you alright, Marnie?" asked a concerned Jimmy. She smiled up at him.

"When you're out here for a while trudging along, you have a lot of time to think. You have time to relive and remember things," she declared. Her manner was unusually tender and seductive. "About a half mile back on the trail it occurred to me that I owed you something from a week ago." He looked back at her in a confused manner. "We're out here in the open with a fresh breeze to keep the bugs away. Why don't you relax here on the ground and let me repay you for everything you've done for me? She eased Jimmy onto his back and methodically removed his manhood from inside his pants.

"Here? Now? In public?" he asked. Her aggressive gesture left him flustered. His reaction caused her to chuckle.

"Not exactly in public. My God, we haven't passed another hiker in an hour and a half." Although anxious at first, he eventually relaxed and enjoyed her attention. The lover's time spent on the ledge lasted a quarter of an hour and further cemented the relationship. They returned home to Wells on Monday night but only after visiting numerous antique shops along the way.

Marion's return home to Wells Beach would have proven anticlimactic if it had not been for the message from her ex-husband blinking on her answering machine. The rambling message from Monty asked her if she would not reconsider taking their daughter for the summer. No doubt, Mia had enlisted her father to act on her behalf, she thought. Marion, still basking in the afterglow of her weekend in Bar Harbor, returned the call immediately and informed her ex-husband that this would be impossible given the new direction in her life. When he dared ask her to be more specific she refused, indicating that her privacy was now something she valued greatly. It was at that point in the conversation that she abruptly, borderline rudely, brought it to an end. Hanging up the phone, she drew in a deep breath and internalized the status of her new life. Not only was Jimmy Sullivan bringing personal companionship and sexual gratification to her in this new life she was forging, he was providing her with the strength to deal with the residue of her past, shattered existence.

Chapter 7

Marion was resting on her oceanside porch, a novel perched in her lap, when Mia's Honda rolled into her driveway on the far side of the house. After placing a bookmarker into the novel, she rose to her feet and made the short walk around the cottage to greet her daughter. The pretty brunette teenager emerged from the compact car and rushed toward her mother. Even at first glance, Marion observed that Mia had gained a few pounds since she had last been with her. Her daughter had been quite slender all through high school and right into college. Marion beamed a smile and threw open her arms.

"My baby," she exclaimed, grabbing hold of the college student and hugging her enthusiastically. "I can't believe we've let this much time pass," she added. Mia Bell was an attractive girl with short, brown hair that draped a pair of deep, blue eyes. Tall like her mother, she also bore a facial resemblance to Marion.

"Don't look too closely at me. I may have avoided the freshman fifteen unlike so many kids, but I seem to have put on the sophomore ten," the girl announced, a reference to the weight gain her mother had already detected.

"You look marvelous," proclaimed Marion in her best Billy Crystal impersonation. "But, if you do think you could afford to drop a few pounds, I think we can take care of that in the next week," bragged Marion. "Ten pounds is nothing." Mia was then led into the house by her mother.

"The house looks great," announced the teenager while peeling off a light sweater and making herself at home in the living room. Not one to get hung up on formality, the girl slipped off her sneakers and curled up into a ball on the couch.

"Diet Moxie?" asked Marion from the doorway.

"Really?"

"Hey kid, when in Maine," she answered.

"Sure, why not?" Marion plucked two bottles from the refrigerator and joined her daughter in the back room of the house. Mother and daughter sat quietly for the next few moments, both seemingly glad to fidget with their soda bottle. Looking across the room, Marion thought the teenager was eager to initiate a discussion. "I'm a little surprised you haven't asked me about things with dad," blurted out the girl after downing a swig of soda.

"What's there to ask about? Your father has his new life and I have mine."

"I know he felt bad, we both did, when we heard you had lost your job," said

Mia, seeming to wander off topic.

"No one felt worse than I did kid," answered her mother dryly. Mia's eyes dropped to the floor.

"Things have gotten really, really bad at home," announced the girl. "Momma, she has daddy running around like a twenty-year-old and he looks ridiculous. She doesn't work anymore. She only had to hint that her job was depressing her and he insisted that she quit. Now, Morina spends all her time at the gym or at the coffee shop with her idiot friends while daddy works away and then tries to keep up with her in the evening." Marion listened intently to her daughter's account of Monty's new life. She knew it was wrong of her, but she could not help obtain a certain sadistic pleasure from the update.

"She's young. She may very well grow out of it," injected Marion judiciously, not believing a word of her own assessment.

"That's never going to happen. Morina is a witch and it's like daddy is under her spell."

"Darling, you have to understand, men have been led down this path by wily females since the beginning of time. There is almost nothing we can do about it. In the end, for better or for worse, it will work itself out," she added. Mia closed her eyes, a pained expression plastered across her face.

"She isn't even pretty if you ask me," proclaimed the teenager.

"No sweetheart, she is. She is quite pretty. I got a glimpse of her before one of those meetings down at the lawyer's office. She is what's referred to as a femme fatale. There are pretty women and there are beautiful women...and then there are femme fatales. They have something beyond looks. They have an animal magnetism that men, men like your father, cannot resist." Marion recognized that her words were only depressing and unnerving her daughter. "Daughter dear, enough of this talk. Why don't you go back to the car and unload your luggage? After that you can get settled and maybe around six I'll treat you to dinner at Billy's Chowder House? Mia nodded her head in acceptance. The teenager rose from the couch and turned toward the door.

"Oh, have you seen much of the Sullivans this spring?" she asked.

"Only Jimmy. Jerry and May went on some grand tour or cruise this year and Jimmy sort of inherited the house for the summer," she reported. She was careful not to mention Jimmy's run of disappointments this year. She reckoned that was his to share or withhold from her daughter over the next week.

It was a few minutes after six o'clock when Mia descended the stairs and joined her mother in the living room. Both were dressed for dinner. Marion was in the process of hunting down her car keys when Jimmy Sullivan materialized outside the screen door to the porch. It was apparent he had just finished work, his shirt drenched from perspiration and his hair matted across his forehead.

"Mrs. Bell, any chance you could spare a cold one for a poor, worn out manual laborer?" he called into the house. Marion was immediately struck by the formal salutation. Jimmy had not called her Mrs. Bell in nearly a month.

"Hi Jimmy," called out Mia. "Long time, no see." Jimmy feigned surprise.

"Oh, Mia. That's right. I don't think you even came up to Wells last summer," he exclaimed. "I'd give you a neighborly hug but I'm a filthy mess and you two lovely ladies look like you're going out for the evening," he added.

"I'm afraid I've been using Jimmy like an unpaid hired hand since I arrived last month," piped in Marion. "Why don't you just go out to the kitchen and serve yourself? You'll have to settle for a Guinness and not that puddle water I usually see you drinking," she added. Jimmy shook Mia's hand before sending Marion a warm, sideways glance and exiting the room. "There are cold cuts in the fridge if you're hungry called out Marion before mother and daughter cleared the front door and descended the stairs to the car.

It was no more than a two-minute drive from their front door on Atlantic Avenue to the parking lot at Billy's Chowder House. Both mother and daughter were visibly becoming more relaxed in each other's company.

"Mom, first, I have to say that you look terrific. I've never seen you looking this physically fit before. What is it, the seafood?" Marion broke out laughing.

"No darling, I think it's called the stress and loneliness diet, but I wouldn't recommend it. Actually, I've been doing a lot of walking along the beach in addition to following the Atkins Diet. The combination of those two has done the trick. In truth, I was only eleven pounds over my goal when I arrived, so it wasn't some miraculous accomplishment," she explained.

"It was nice seeing Jimmy again. He looks good…really good," confessed the teenager.

"He's a handsome boy," added Marion while her mind flashed back to the mountain ledge in Bar Harbor.

"Do you know if he's seeing anyone?" Marion struggled to remain poised and seemingly half-interested.

"Yes, there seems to be someone but, then again, that's not something he would be likely to share with me." *Please darling, change the subject.* The nineteen-year-old stared out the car window toward the horizon.

"It's funny, I don't think he ever thought of me seriously in a romantic way because of the age difference. When you are in your teens, three years is a big difference. But, if he were to show any interest while I'm here then I certainly wouldn't play hard to get. I just don't remember him being this good looking," she admitted. The car was slowing down while Marion prepared to leave Mile Road and pull into the parking lot. The teenager broke into giddy laughter and placed her hand on her mother's shoulder. "Oh, to be twenty years younger, huh?"

Chapter 8

It was Friday night. The weekend had arrived. Jimmy had made himself scarce since the evening of Mia's arrival. Marion was returning from a walk south to Fisherman's Cove and thought she picked up on a familiar face approaching. After learning of her plans from Mia, Jimmy had headed southward to intercept her. He needed some private time with her.

"Are you being followed?" Marion called out in jest.

"I don't think so. I slithered off when I heard her on the phone. Your daughter's arrival just sort of came on us and I wanted to get your take on just how to conduct myself."

"This is a little uncomfortable. I won't even go into how the conversation went the other night at Billy's. However, we had to expect this. Just so you know, my daughter thinks you are kind of a cool guy, just like her mother does. Now, I know this might be a lot to ask but is there any chance you could make yourself even more scarce for the next few days? Nothing too obvious but maybe just hard to come by?"

"That's what I've been doing. I've had the shades down on your side of the house and, if you've noticed, I've been out until nearly midnight both days." Marion leaned against her lover, dropping her head onto his shoulder.

"You've been more than great. She knows the clock is ticking, after a week and it's back to Connecticut. We can't make this avoidance thing too obvious. Mia's not stupid. She'll start putting the puzzle pieces together if we're not careful," Marion cautioned. She broke contact and Jimmy responded with a passionate kiss on the lips. She lifted her right hand, placing it on the side of his face. "I am beyond fortunate to have you," she declared.

It was after seven-thirty on Friday night when Jimmy wandered into the Beachcomber Gift Shop on Wells Beach and casually strolled the aisles in search of a few tee shirts to add to his casual wardrobe. He was stationed in the far corner of the store when he lifted his eyes to the sound of the door opening and spied the entrance of Mia Bell. Trapped between the pretty teenager and the door, he moved to a spot partially blinded by a display of sweat shirts. Carol, the owner, greeted the girl with a burst of southern Maine hospitality and a short checklist of sale items while Jimmy jockeyed to remain out of sight. Mia's eyes flashed around the showroom of spring and summer clothing before settling on stacks of hooded sweatshirts by the wall. With her attention fixed on a variety of hoodies, Sullivan moved out from behind a display and quietly moved forward in the direction of the front door. Halfway to the door, he glanced over and saw Mia begin a slow turn in his direction. He turned from her and dropped his eyes down on the merchandise table by the picture window. Oh great, female bathing suits and skimpy ones at that. Just what a healthy, American male should be checking out in his spare time. He glanced over his shoulder to see the shop owner, Carol, taking him in. She shot him a mischievous grin and looked away. Knowing he could not linger any longer in place, he turned and stepped closer to the store entrance. Outside, a chorus of shouts from a passing group of teenage boys caused Mia's head to lurch upward and toward the front of the building.

"Hey Jimmy, our paths finally cross again. Mom said that you've been pretty much out straight lately, but I was hoping to get a chance to see you again before I headed back to Connecticut. We're planning on whipping up something Italian for dinner tomorrow night and we'd love to have you over. You'd be doing our family a big favor. I don't think mom is mixing enough with people since everything crashed in on her last year and every little bit would help," declared the girl, her blue eyes sparkling above a youthful, innocent smile. Jimmy lifted his eyes to the ceiling in search of a credible excuse.

"Maybe in a couple of weeks," he offered. *Wow, that was lame. She knows that you know she won't be around in a couple of weeks.* Her expression broke into an exaggerated frown.

"It almost sounds like someone is intentionally trying to avoid me," she complained. "Again, you would be doing the whole family a favor. From what I can gather, my mother is just sort of hiding away up here and walking the beach alone every day like a hermit. Please, it would mean the world to me." Sullivan gazed into the girl's eyes and saw the sincerity embedded in her plea. He was also aware that any further resistance to her simple request might raise questions to his motive.

"Okay, for the family. The Bells and the Sullivans go back a long way here at Wells Beach. Just give me a time and I'll make a point of being there," he conceded.

"Why don't you plan on coming over around seven. Informal attire will be appropriate," answered the delighted teenager.

News of the dinner guest reached Marion on Mia's return from shopping. She feigned ambivalence to the news, not wanting to provide her daughter with even the hint of discomfort. The giddy teenager recounted the happenchance of running into Jimmy Sullivan at the Beachcomber before coming clean to her mother.

"I spotted Jimmy's car parked right outside the shop and figured there was a good chance he was inside," confessed the girl. "It came off without a hitch and I'm sure he's clueless. I made it seem so coincidental," she added. Strewn out along the couch, Marion extended her daughter an unenthusiastic smile. *My little girl seems to be developing her feminine wiles right on schedule. It seems like only yesterday when she was rushing around before her first dance and now look at her. No doubt, Jimmy will come to me with an account of how, out of pure bad timing, he ran into Mia at the Beachcomber and now finds himself forced into this dinner engagement. I almost feel sorry for men sometime. Little do they realize how many of life's little coincidences are just the handiwork of some scheming female.*

"Any suggestions on what to serve?" Marion asked.

"I told him it would probably be Italian."

"Well, there goes my Atkins Diet," cracked Marion. "We can go with spaghetti and meatballs and I'll just take it easy on the pasta and binge on the meatballs." Mia nodded her approval.

"Mother, the next time you go out on one of your walks would you let me know so I can join you? I can clearly see that all that exercise has done you a lot of good and I wouldn't mind jumping on that band wagon for a while," confessed the pretty brunette. Her mother nodded yes. *This is exactly what I prayed not to happen. Mia's clearly developing some sort of feelings for Jimmy. Thank God, we're talking seven days then off she goes.*

Chapter 9

Jimmy Sullivan appeared at the porch door of the Bell house at precisely seven o'clock on Saturday night with a humble bouquet of flowers in hand. It was Marion who greeted him. Mia was still upstairs fussing over herself with hopes of ultimately making a grand entrance. The few moments alone at the door allowed the twenty-two-year old to passionately kiss his lover for the first time in days, a gesture greatly appreciated by the woman. They locked eyes for a pregnant moment, both clearly not looking forward to the next few hours. No words were spoken nor had to be. From the floor above came the shuffling of footsteps toward the stairwell. Mia was about to join them.

On this evening, Jimmy was treated as a guest with Marion and Mia functioning as co-hostesses. True to her word, Marion limited her pasta intake and abstained from the basket of garlic bread served with the meal. All three drank their share of wine and the conversation was lively and, for the better part of the evening, kept on matters of substance. Above the sound of human voices there was heard the whistle of the wind as an off-shore storm brought gusts in off the crashing surf outside their door. Two hours after the start of the meal and just after the dessert dishes had been cleared the threesome withdrew to the parlor. Almost from habit, Jimmy claimed a spot at the end of the couch and was joined immediately by Mia. Last to arrive in the room, Marion found herself seated in her usual chair of choice by the door to the porch. All three were nursing their fourth or fifth glass of wine. Settled in place, Jimmy extended Marion an affectionate, albeit discreet, glance just before Mia came forth with a contented sigh and rested her head on his shoulder. Marion looked on uncomfortably, numbed by the awkward circumstances while struggling to somehow normalize her surroundings.

"Jimmy…any word from your parents?" she asked.

"As a matter of fact, there was an email yesterday. They were curious to know if I had somehow gotten my budding professional career on track from their home here on the edge of the Atlantic Ocean, the operative words being their home," he answered sarcastically.

"Where are your parents?" asked Mia.

"They're on this grand tour of Europe and parts of Asia. They won't be back until early August. They're celebrating their twenty-fifth wedding anniversary."

"It must be costing them a fortune," injected Mia from her comfortable position resting against their guest. Jimmy ignored her statement.

"They will probably come right up to Maine on their return. That's not a reunion I will be looking forward to," he confessed listlessly. The conversation continued for another half hour. During this interlude, Mia managed to casually, almost effortlessly, drape her arm over Jimmy's shoulder, her finger playing with the collar of his shirt. *Oh my God, Jimmy looks so uncomfortable. My daughter seems to have picked up some intimacy moves in college. I'd be a little jealous if he didn't look so uneasy.* It was a few minutes short of eleven o'clock when Marion ushered the evening to a close and initiated Jimmy's return home.

"Mom, why don't you go on upstairs to bed. I'll escort Jimmy to the door and then pick up the kitchen before joining you up there?" Mia suggested. Marion was not pleased with her daughter's cunning maneuver but acquiesced to the suggestion. She did not want to give Mia any reason to suspect the new reality in her mother's life. She climbed the stairs to her bedroom, trying to imagine what manner of seductive charm her daughter could be exposing Jimmy to and, in turn, how he was weathering the storm. *She's leaving next Wednesday and that's carved in stone. No excuses or delays or extensions to further bond with her mother or Mr. Sullivan. I love my daughter but she's gone if I have to fly her out of Portland myself.*

On the morning of Mia's departure, mother and daughter were seated at the kitchen table sharing a breakfast of western omelets when the nineteen-year-old confided in her.

"I kissed Jimmy Sullivan on Saturday night before he left for the evening," she confessed between bites of her meal. "And it wasn't some innocent kiss, it was intense. I wasn't going to take no for an answer. He hesitated but I knew he'd give in. He may still think of me as a kid, but I know it made an impact on him. Mom, I literally felt his legs grow weak a second or two into it," she bragged. The revelation sent a shockwave through Marion's stomach.

"You can't be leading the boy on," she counseled. "He's already had his heart broken once in the last year."

"No, I wouldn't do that. To be honest, I really like Jimmy. If you weren't tossing me out, I'd be hanging around a lot longer." The girl looked up at her mother and put on a comical frown. Marion held her ground.

"Your place is back in Connecticut where your father needs you. There's no telling what his young hussy might get him to do without you to talk sense to him."

It was Saturday morning and Marion found herself woefully low on groceries. Three days had passed since Mia's departure and Jimmy had not raised the matter of her daughter's passionate kiss in conversation. Jimmy had decided to join Marion on her visit to the grocery store. In the past, she shopped at the local IGA up on Route 1 and this day was no exception. She liked the store. It reminded her of the supermarket in her hometown back in Connecticut. She was particularly fond of the fresh fruits and vegetables there and spent her first ten minutes in the store meandering through the fresh produce. Presently, Marion stood in the aisle displaying canned fruit. Jimmy was away by the meat counter selecting items contained on a list provided to him. She was deep in thought when a male voice broke her concentration.

"It is such a tough decision. Do you buy the name brand and stick with the familiar or do you pick up the house brand and save thirty cents?" She lifted her eyes from the can of Mandarin oranges clutched in her hand. Standing beside her was a silver-haired gentleman sporting a white mustache and dressed in casual clothing. "I mean it's only a quarter difference in price but a quarter here and a quarter there and it really starts to add up," he declared.

"Oh my God, does my poverty show that much?" clowned Marion before laughing politely.

"A penny saved is a penny earned," continued the man.

"Astute observations and clichés too. You definitely know how to charm a girl, stranger," she declared as the two continued their banter.

"Actually, I may be a stranger to you but you're not a stranger to me. I see you, quite often, walking along the beach in Wells." She nodded her head knowingly.

"That would be me. I do spend a lot of time walking along the shore and contemplating the meaning of life." The man continued to smile at her, his eyes combing her face in apparent appreciation.

"And what's your verdict?" he asked.

"Is this old geezer bothering you, Marion?" asked Jimmy from behind the man, his testosterone on full display in his words and posture. Startled, the stranger turned to confront the twenty-two-year old then immediately thought better of it.

"Down boy. Jimmy, this man is being anything but impolite or rude. We were only trading comments concerning the meaning of life and Mandarin oranges," explained Marion laughingly. "No, I think you may owe this gentleman an apology," she added firmly. Jimmy Sullivan exhaled and visibly attempted to quell his anger. A few, uncomfortable seconds passed before he forced out a response.

"My apologies about the harsh words, my mistake," he finally muttered. His words lacked any hint of sincerity.

"Apology accepted but I'm afraid that, at the age of fifty-nine, it could take a while to recover from the old geezer comment," he confessed. Marion smiled up at the gentleman and reached out her hand. The confrontation unnerved her and she needed to move past it as quickly as possible. The stranger shook hands and smiled meekly before turning away. The incident was behind her and she would deal with Jimmy in the privacy of the car, she thought.

Marion counted out her payment for groceries while Jimmy stood quietly by the carriage. The transaction completed he followed her into the parking lot and unloaded the half dozen grocery bags into the trunk of her car. Joining her inside the vehicle, he waited on the turn of the car key. When it did not come he glanced across the front seat and saw his lover's eyes riveted on him. He looked away.

"What the hell was that bullshit back there in the store? Are you goddamn insane?" she asked. He rolled his eyes to heaven but did not utter a word in defense of his actions. "I don't even know the Jimmy Sullivan I saw back there in the store." He shook his head from side to side.

"That wasn't me. I don't know who the hell that was," he answered. "I just saw you talking to another man and I lost it."

"Do you honestly believe that I'm going to turn away from you for a guy who might even pass for my father? What else am I in store for? Are you going to tackle the next fifty-year-old who smiles at me on the street?" Marion continued to glare over at her young lover.

"Lesson learned," muttered Jimmy. Continuing to peer across the car, she was taken with a certain submissiveness in his manner. *This is the same virile, young man who intimidated that poor slob back in the store twenty minutes ago and look at him now. Here he is letting a female browbeat him into silence and acceptance. Such is the power of sex and passion and gender that I can carry this off without almost no effort. It makes the very notion of the weaker sex seem laughable.*

"Let's hope so," she concluded. "Now, let's enjoy the rest of the day together with this permanently in our past."

The groceries had all been unpacked and stored in the kitchen cabinets when Jimmy lumbered into Marion's living room and collapsed onto the couch. Picking up the television remote, he clicked on the set and went in search of a sporting event, any sporting event. He was joined a few minutes later by Marion. Making her way across the room, she claimed the same chair she had sat in one week earlier following dinner.

"What is that, soccer?" she called out. He nodded yes. She rose to her feet, walked across the room and snatched up the remote. In less than a second the television went silent. Football, baseball, basketball and hockey are for men. Soccer is for wimps," she proclaimed before tossing the remote across the room onto a nearby chair. Returning to her original chair of choice, she stared at him seductively.

"Okay crazy woman, what now?" Marion reached down, removed one and then the other of her flats, and tossed them across the room at him. He caught the first but mishandled the second. It struck him on the chest. Rising to her feet, she walked to the oceanside wall and closed the Venetian blinds, leaving any beachside pedestrians without a view into the house. She proceeded to unbutton her blouse and toss it in his direction. He made no attempt to catch the garment and it came to rest in his lap. Marion stepped toward him and seated herself on the coffee table directly in front of the couch. She removed her bra in slow motion before flipping it at Jimmy. It landed draped over his right shoulder. *I can't believe I'm doing this, but I must erase all memory he has of sitting here next to Mia. He's not laughing so I'm probably not making a total fool of myself.* She dropped her feet to the floor and stood, the upper half of her body naked. Pausing dramatically for a second, she then slipped off her jeans and buried his head inside of them. Her young lover made no effort to escape or uncover his face. She mounted his lap clothed only in her panties and kissed him through the denim fabric, finding his mouth behind the crotch of her jeans. "At this moment in time, you own me," he confessed. His words caused her to giggle. She folded back a flap of denim, allowing her mouth to find his bare lips. She kissed him with intensity and felt his body surrender under her weight.

"I have a bit of a confession to make to you," she purred into his ear. He did not respond to her words, appearing to be in a state of elevated ecstasy. "A small part of me got turned on when you threatened that poor slob at the market. You were ready to take this guy apart for me and there is something sexually primal and arousing about that," she declared before plunging her tongue deep inside his mouth. Marion sat atop her young lover feeling his temperature rise and body grow hard. She was in total control of him at this moment in time and they both knew it. "Now, we are both going upstairs to my bed and I am going to suck the very life out of you," she asserted. Incredibly, she thought she could literally feel the impact of her words in his body beneath her. She rose up from atop her willing victim and helped him to his feet. The two lovers spent the entire Saturday afternoon isolated alone in Marion's bedroom while a steady stream of tourists walked, ran and played on the edge of the Atlantic Ocean below. Marion ended the day convinced that all memory of her daughter had been, for all intents and purposes, erased from Jimmy Sullivan's memory.

Chapter 10

Summer arrived in southern Maine with its share of unwanted baggage, bumper to bumper traffic snarls along Route 1 and an overabundance of scantily clad Canadian tourists clogging the aisles in grocery stores and clothed in outfits both ill-fitted and ill-advised for them. Early summer was good to Marion. By the second week of July she was sporting a healthy-looking tan which even appeared to shave a few more years from her appearance. Her combination diet and exercise regimen managed to bring her weight down to just over one hundred and thirty pounds. All this and a boyfriend twenty-five- years her junior meant that she was living the dream. Marion was just about to prepare herself a sandwich when she heard the porch door open in the next room.

"I need a beer," announced Jimmy while entering the kitchen and before planting a kiss on his lover's neck. Not waiting on an invitation, he proceeded to the refrigerator and snatched a bottle from the top shelf.

"Can I make you a sandwich?" she asked.

"No, I've already eaten," he replied impatiently. "I just came from McDonalds where I've suffered psychological torture at the hands of one of our visitors from the north." His words caused her to chuckle. "I had the misfortune of being in line behind this Canadian who struggled with the language. This middle-aged slug was standing in line in front of me and staring up at the menu sign…the sign that doesn't just spell out the name of the sandwich but also provides a picture of it ten times its actual size."

"Careful with that middle-aged talk," cautioned the woman over a pair of reading glasses. Jimmy raised his hand defensively and acknowledged his mistake.

"Anyway, Pierre just stood there in front of me with his mouth open and a stupefied expression on his face trying to comprehend if the oversized picture of a Big Mac did, indeed, represent the sandwich of the same name. He just stood there for what seemed like five minutes holding up the line. Oh, and to make matters worse, he stood there in nothing but a shirt over his bathing trunks, barefoot and with sand plastered on his legs and feet. Marion, I swear, I just wanted to haul off and slug him it pissed me off so much," howled Jimmy. "This jerk was just so incredibly rude." Having completed the preparation of her sandwich, Marion calmly claimed a chair at the kitchen table and took the first bite of her evening meal. His tirade over, Jimmy stood patiently sipping his beer and waiting on her response.

"My darling, that was truly a pathetic display put on by Pierre. That's what you said his name was, Pierre?"

"That's the name I gave the inconsiderate bastard."

"Well, your criticism of this dimwit is probably justified but the truly pathetic thing here does not lie with him but actually with you and every other male within a hundred miles of here," she explained.

"What are you talking about?"

"What I'm talking about is that you got all bent out of shape by some dope of a tourist who wasted your time at McDonalds. Now, based on your description, I think it's safe to say that this guy would never be mistaken for Tom Brady or Brad Pitt. Am I right?" Jimmy nodded in agreement. "What I'm saying is that instead of being Pierre the idiot, the person in question was some little French-Canadian eyeful with a tight, little ass and a pair of legs that went on forever? Would Jimmy Sullivan have been the same impatient hard ass that I see standing before me or an accommodating putz, laughing along with the sexy little visitor from the north and maybe even offering to brush some of that nasty, old beach sand from her long, smooth legs?" asked Marion in a mockingly, high voice. Jimmy choked up a mouthful of beer through laughter while shaking his head feverishly.

"No freaking way," he called out to her and half of Atlantic Avenue.

"Mademoiselle, please, let me brush all that sand from your feet and carry your food order out to the car for you. It is truly an honor being kept waiting for a person like yourself," she continued in jest while he tried unsuccessfully to subdue his laughter. A moment later he as waving off her comical barrage.

"You've managed to get me out of my bad mood but some bad news from home hasn't gone away," he declared. Marion's face turned serious while she searched his for a clue to his secret.

"I heard from my parents a few minutes ago. They're due back home the first or second week of August and they plan on coming up to Wells for a visit almost immediately. Based on what my dad was saying, they're planning to light a fire under me. It sounds like they expect me out interviewing for a job immediately." Marion's eyes dropped in reaction to his news and she placed her sandwich down. "It sounds like they plan to throw me out of the house," he added. I kind of knew this or something like this was bound to happen sooner or later.

"You can't fault them for this, Jimmy. They love you and they probably think that a little tough love is in order," she suggested.

"Hey, it's not like I don't plan on putting my education to work for me. It's just that I'd like to have at least one summer to kick back and chill a little," he reasoned.

"And this thing between us. You certainly can't be thinking of telling them about us, can you?" she asked. Jimmy looked down at Marion. His disposition had turned deadly serious.

"If it were just me and you hadn't known the family for years, I would come right out and tell them. But, I think you're against anything like that. Am I right?" She nodded yes and took a bite from her sandwich.

"We can work through whatever comes down the pike at us. You know I'll make room for you right here in the house if it comes to that. I wouldn't want you staying here while your folks were next door but at any other time," confided Marion. Jimmy moved forward, stopping just above her. He gestured for her to rise. She followed his direction and a second later they were embraced in a kiss. Pulling away slightly, she traced his lips with the tip of her tongue. "We have to make the most of every minute and second this summer," she insisted. Her twenty-two-year old lover pulled her back into an embrace, his actions confirming her words.

Summer droned on and the days and nights grew warmer and increasingly humid. Jimmy was now routinely spending the night with Marion and taking advantage of the powerful air conditioner wedged under her bedroom window. It was a Tuesday morning in the dying days of July. Jimmy emerged from the three-quarter bath adjacent to the bedroom and bid his lover a good day.

"Oh Jimmy, when you come home from work this afternoon would you forsake your obligatory shower and just find me?" Marion asked. "I have a strong suspicion that I'm going to feel dirty later today if you get my drift."

"I'll make a note of it," he answered lightheartedly. "Oh Marnie, in case I forgot to mention it, I'll be heading out Friday night for Hartford. I have a buddy from high school that's getting married and I feel obligated to be there," he reported. "We were pretty close our junior and senior years and I signed on to go back for this thing in March." He looked down on his lover who was observing him curiously. He broke eye contact. "The wedding and reception is down smack dab in my old stomping grounds…and my parent's stomping grounds," he added.

"Totally understandable," answered Marion before rolling over and pulling the bedsheets up over her naked body.

Marion lay outstretched on her porch hammock and watched as beachgoers traipsed the mile of beach extending from the bottom of Mile Road up to the granite jetty guarding the opening to Wells Harbor. She was alone this weekend with Jimmy a hundred miles away attending a wedding in Connecticut. It was a hazy and hot day causing perspiration to bead on her forehead and neck. She took a sip from a glass of Diet Moxie and critically examined her lower body. *I look damn good for a woman of forty-seven. Lightly tanned and as slender as I was my freshman year of college. My God, it won't be that long until we're marking the one-year anniversary of the attack. Yes, it's been a bitch of a year, but I've come through it okay. The good Lord gave me lemons, but I just made lemonade…gallons and gallons and gallons of lemonade.* Marion chuckled under her breath and closed her eyes. *God, I miss the little shit, but I must remember that he's not going to be around* forever. Maybe this weekend alone is good practice. From the interior of the house came the sound of her cell phone. She groaned and rose to her feet. She found the phone resting on a small table in the front hallway.

"Hello," she said through a partial yawn.

"Hey mom, how's it going?" It was Mia. "I wouldn't have called so soon since my visit but there's something developing back here at home that I thought you should know about."

"Nothing involving you, I hope," said Marion.

"No, not me. It's dad. He's been seeing one doctor after another this past week and I know they've performed a bunch of tests on him. When I ask him about it, he just shrugs it off, but I can tell he's concerned about things."

"Would you feel better if I gave him a call?" she suggested.

"No, don't do that," answered the anxious teenager. "I think he'd be really pissed at me if he knew I had called you about this. I just want you to be aware of everything going on. It could be nothing, but I just have this bad feeling."

"And what about the trollop? What is her reaction to this possible new reality?"

"Morina hasn't shown any reaction to these new circumstances. Maybe that's a good sign. Dad may be confiding more in her than in me," theorized the teenager.

"Darling, in any event, keep me posted," urged Marion. "Your father may have thrown me out onto the street, but I'd never wish anything serious on him." After exchanging final pleasantries, the conversation was concluded. *She never brought up Jimmy. That's encouraging. She's a kid. No doubt she's already moved on to another hunk closer to home.*

Returning to the porch, Marion stood looking out to sea. The news from Connecticut, as flimsy as it was, upset her. Her mind harkened back to college and the campus party she attended where she first laid eyes on Montgomery Bell. It was half a lifetime ago, she thought. She struggled to put a year on it. *I met Monty back in 1975. God, where is my life going? Everything seems to be just racing forward. My youth is gone. It's past tense. I may have the eye of a young stud at this moment but, it's just that...momentary. I really hope Mia's worrying over nothing. However, the truth is this carefree summer is beginning to turn to shit right before my eyes. In two weeks the Sullivans will arrive. Talk about a pressure packed time at the beach. If word of the affair should come to their attention I'm not sure I'll be able to deal with it. What do you say to a pair of old friends? Sorry folks but I was at a difficult time in my life, so I spent the summer sucking some of the youth out of your son. Again, nothing personal.*

Chapter 11

Jimmy's head lay in Marion's lap while her fingers traced rings through his wavy hair. They were resting on the living room couch while the active Atlantic Ocean surged and receded on the sand only forty feet away. The two lovers were in the final stages of the lull before the storm. The Sullivans were due to arrive at Wells Beach and reclaim their oceanfront house in twenty-four hours.

"We both knew the day would come and here it is staring us in the face," lamented Marion prior to leaning forward and planting a tender kiss on Jimmy's lips. "Are you up for this?" she asked.

"That's pretty much irrelevant. They're going to be here whether I'm ready for them or not." Marion stared down on her lover and scanned his youthful, handsome face. *Tonight could be my last night with Jimmy. Who knows what will come with this pending confrontation with his folks? They could send him packing over the weekend and that will be pretty much the end of that. I knew this was coming. It's not like I didn't know this was doomed from day one. I must embrace tonight for both of our sakes.*

"What if I decided to treat us to dinner? I'm thinking York would be good. I think it's best that we aren't seen out anywhere in Wells on the eve of your parent's return."

"Great idea, but I'd prefer to pay my own way. I agree but also only on the condition we have lots of personal time tonight," he insisted.

"Let's compromise, my dearest. What if I pick up the tab for meal and drinks and you cover the tip?" Jimmy frowned momentarily then shrugged his shoulders.

"It's not perfect but it'll keep me from feeling like a kept man," he concluded.

Marion was in the home stretch of her daily walk when her eyes rested on the oceanside of the Sullivan house and observed three individuals standing close by the porch and seemingly looking out to sea. The moment has arrived, she thought. Jerry and May Sullivan are here to right the ship and get their son back on track. I can't even imagine where our conversations will go. No doubt the question of whether Jimmy has made a nuisance of himself or whether there have been any disturbances next door could come up. What do I say? How mortifying would it be if, by some unforeseeable event, they become aware of the affair?

The Sullivan family had retreated into the house by the time Marion reached her porch. She played with the idea of greeting her old friends on the spot but backed away at the last moment and instead made her way into her own kitchen and opened a bottle of wine. After pouring a glass, she wandered back onto her porch and claimed the hammock. Peering out over the ocean of whitecaps, she settled back and began the process of coming to terms with her new reality. *Okay, the last thing I should do is try to avoid the Sullivans. That's an absolute. On the other hand, I don't think rushing up to their door with open arms is the way to go. For all I know there's some serious discussions involving Jimmy's career going on between the three of them at this very moment. I think it's best for me to just chill out here on the porch in plain sight for an hour or so. I'll let them call me over when they have the inclination.*

Marion stationed herself at the southern end of the porch after retrieving a novel from inside the house. Locking her tanned ankles atop the porch railing, she found her bookmarked page and dove back into the work of fiction. Twenty minutes passed before there came the sound of activity from a short distance away. The three Sullivans had emerged from the house and out onto their oceanside porch. Within moments, Marion had been spotted.

"Marion," called out May Sullivan. The tone of her voice told Marion that word of the affair had not reached the Sullivan's ears. She swiveled her head.

"May…Jerry, it's wonderful to see you both again," she called back. "You've been missed this summer. It's so good to see you again," gushed Marion while lowering her legs and making her way down from the porch and over into her neighbor's yard. Jimmy stood silently behind his parents. Marion made her way up to the couple and exchanged embraces first with May and then Jerry.

"Oh my God, you look terrific," exclaimed May after pushing Marion away to arm's length and looking her up and down. "Look at her, Jerry. Doesn't she look fantastic?" Her husband agreed with a nod of the head but was careful to not match his wife's enthusiasm.

"Jimmy, it's also good to see you again but it's not like we haven't laid eyes on each other since last year," added Marion. The Sullivans invited their neighbor to join them on the porch and she enthusiastically accepted. Marion settled into a wicker chair but turned down the offer of a beverage.

"Please tell us that Jimmy didn't turn himself into another Kramer and try mooching from you morning, noon and night," insisted May while referencing the Seinfeld television comedy. Marion laughed and shot Jimmy an affectionate glance.

"Early on there was a need to provide him with a few cups of coffee but nothing over the top. To be honest, it was nice seeing a friendly face at the door on occasion to break up the day," she confessed. There was a pause in the conversation. She had indirectly brought up the eight-hundred-pound gorilla in the room.

"We were surprised and devastated at the word of you and Monty's divorce.

We had no idea," blurted out Jerry Sullivan. Marion dropped her eyes to the floor.

"These things happen," she stated soberly.

"Mrs. Bell did not look like she does today when I arrived in May. I had the impression she used me to keep herself on track with her exercise program," injected Jimmy, feeling the need to contribute something to the conversation.

"Jimmy's right. I made a point of catching him on the way in or the way out and updating him on my progress," added Marion. *My God, I'm making it sound like the only time we set eyes on each other was getting in and out of our cars. Oh, and is it my imagination or are Jerry's eyes spending an awful lot of the time below my neck? I'm thinking back to those album covers Jimmy told me about. I wonder if he's comparing my body to Michelle Phillips and hearing California Dreamin' playing in his head? I almost wish Jimmy hadn't shared that story with me.*

A short time later the conversation shifted from Marion and Jimmy's dull lives at Wells Beach to the Sullivan's adventure of a lifetime exploring the continent of Europe and the waters of the Mediterranean Sea. Marion feigned enraptured interest in the couple's account of their adventure knowing that time spent describing their travels was time not spent gathering information on the details of their son's summer. In the end, the sun was just setting behind the tree line on the far side of Route 1 when Marion excused herself and returned to her darkened house. Flooding her living room with artificial light, she was happy with her decision to meet with the Sullivans early after their arrival and even more happy with her performance as the jilted, middle-aged divorcee who has somehow managed to survive a good part of the summer alone at the shore.

If Marion thought she might be spending the weekend alone, she was wrong. By ten o'clock Saturday morning, a day of shopping, new and antique, had already been planned by May Sullivan and her. The two friends lunched in the harbor district of Portland and spent the remainder of the afternoon visiting a wide array of shops populating the immediate, downtown area. Marion presumed that Jimmy was spending the afternoon with his father and possibly hashing out the direction the recent graduate's life might take. All the while, Marion was careful to not bring up her young lover's name out of fear of slipping up and referencing a suspicious detail of the past two months. Again, as she was the evening before, she was content to allow her neighbor to relate experiences from abroad in minute detail with the knowledge that the time spent listening to the adventures of the elder Sullivans was time not spent considering the nature of the junior Sullivan's social life away from college and home.

"We're not sure what the next step will be in guiding Jimmy back on track," confessed May on the drive back to Wells and York County. "One possibility is that we get him into graduate school this fall. We know it's a little late, but Jerry is pretty sure he can pull a few strings and maybe call in a couple of favors," indicated May, her tone now more serious than earlier in the day. "All we know is that we cannot let things move forward on their own." Marion remained silent. "We know Jimmy would prefer to stay in Wells until, at least, Labor Day but this is not convenient for us. We have professional friends who are interested in renting the house and after what we just shelled out in Europe the money could be put to good use," explained the Sullivan woman. "Also, if we go the graduate school route then there's more money we'll have to come up with." Marion glanced across the front seat of the car.

"May, if there's anything I can do to help you two out then please don't be afraid to ask," offered Marion. "I have two extra bedrooms and I'm not expecting to see Mia again until sometime in October." *There it is May. I've dropped it in your lap. I'll be damned if I make the offer. No May, you're going to make the offer for me. Would I mind if Jimmy stayed with me for the next two or three weeks? Ask me.*

"Marion, I know this must look bad on the surface, like we came up here just to say hello and then abuse our friendship but if it wouldn't be too much to ask?" Marion sneaked a peak over at her friend and neighbor. May Sullivan appeared embarrassed.

"It's not too much to ask at all," she answered. Reaching across the front seat of the car, she squeezed the woman's hand. *No doubt, I'm going to burn in hell for this someday. This is something like Erica Kane would do but Susan Lucci won't have to go to hell for it. Just me.*

"Jerry handles all of the finances so I don't know how much we'll be taking in from the beach rental, but it has to be two or three grand per week. We don't expect you to do this for nothing. Our longstanding friendship is worth more than a few dollars. Marion grew outwardly uncomfortable. *Oh, sweet Jesus, now you're just playing with me. This is brutal.*

"No, May, please don't go there. It is not an imposition. I don't want anything for this small favor and I'll be insulted if either of you bring it up again," she insisted. "Besides, it will be nice having the company." *Okay, that should do it. I'll be burning in hell someday.*

The two women spent the remainder of the ride back to Wells Beach ironing out the details. Marion could sense her neighbor's relief at finding a place for her son to stay the remainder of the summer season. It was agreed that Jimmy would reimburse Marion for the approximate cost of the food and drink he consumed until his return to Connecticut. By the time Marion reached the Wells and Ogunquit exit off the Maine Turnpike, she had pretty much digested everything that was now in place. *So, from now until Jimmy's return home he will be free to come and go into the house without fear of suspicion. All we must guard against are any overt demonstrations of affection outside the four walls of the house. I guess that also means keeping the blinds down and curtains pulled on the Sullivan house's side of the cottage. My God, I do think we're golden.*

It was Sunday night. Marion was outstretched on the porch with a new novel cradled in her lap while the tidewater surged up to within twenty feet of the house. She was in a state of complete relaxation thanks to the glass of pink wine set within arm's length of the hammock. The high tide had driven most all the beach walkers back onto Atlantic Avenue and left her alone with her ocean. Thirty minutes into her book came the sound of a door closing. She looked up and caught sight of Jimmy Sullivan turning the corner of the house and bounding up onto her porch, a red backpack perched atop his shoulder.

"Well Mrs. Bell, I guess this might be a good time to be appraised of your house rules," he muttered sophomorically. "Oh, and I do hope my bedroom has an ocean view," he added.

"I consider it the best in the house," answered Marion. "And to borrow a line from the movie, *Grease, the rules are there ain't no rules,*" she wisecracked.

"That movie I am familiar with," he reassured her. She rose to her feet and led him inside the house.

"Do you hear that? There ain't no rules," repeated Marion before kissing her young boarder on the mouth. "We have two more weeks, three weeks tops before the most wonderful summer of my life comes to an end. Why don't we go upstairs to our bedroom and celebrate what we have left?" she asked. In the next second, Jimmy's mouth found his lover's neck and he gently drew upon her soft skin. He stared into her eyes as they climbed the stairs to their lair for the next fortnight. The idea of 'no rules' would govern their actions and behavior until the Labor Day weekend when reality tolled an end to the summer of shameful pleasure and ushered in the return, for Marion Bell, of the ordinary and mundane.

Chapter 12

For Marion, the last two weeks of August sped by like a brakeless freight train barreling by a series of crowded terminals. On each day she attempted to hamper the progression of time with predictable results. It was late morning on the Sunday of Labor Day weekend. She was seated in the living room half listening to the talking heads on cable news while Jimmy still lay in bed a floor above the room. A pall had begun descending over the house the previous day, no doubt from the knowledge of Jimmy's imminent departure the following week. The ringing of the phone brought her out of a light nap.

"Hello, Bell residence," she answered in an uncharacteristically formal manner.

"Hi mom, it's Mia. Have I called at a bad time?"

"No dear, not at all. My God, you caught me dosing off and I don't think it's even noon yet. I must be getting old. What's up?"

"Oh Christ, I wish I wasn't calling with bad news but I'm afraid I am," acknowledged her daughter. Marion felt a nervous lump form in the pit of her stomach.

"What is it sweetheart?"

"It's about dad. I'm afraid the doctors have come back with some terrible news," answered the teenager. Partially relieved the news did not involve her daughter, Marion felt the stressful knot within her ease. She let out an audible sigh. "They say he has cancer. It's something to do with his thyroid. It's been weeks since he's been himself, his energy I mean. His primary care doctor kept telling him it wasn't this and it wasn't that and having one test after another done. Once he even went so far to suggest that trying to satisfy a younger woman could be part of the problem. Anyway, dad finally visited another doctor for a second opinion and that's when this whole thyroid cancer came out." Mia paused at the other end of the phone.

"Have they begun treatments yet?" asked a stunned Marion.

"The doctor, the new doctor, told me that dad's case is very advanced and…." Mia stopped in mid-sentence and burst into tears. It took a few seconds for the girl to regain her composure. "He said that daddy's case was so advanced that it was best that we started making him as comfortable as possible. He said that we should not get our hopes up for a recovery," reported the girl. Marion sunk back against the kitchen wall and attempted to fully contemplate her daughter's words.

"And what about that girl, Morina? How is she handling the news?"

"Morina moved out of the house and temporarily back with her folks over a week ago. She is such a bitch. When daddy tried to turn to her for help all she had to say was that she hadn't signed up for this shit and packed her bags," spat out the bitter daughter. Marion took a deep breath while the circumstances of the moment sent her mind spinning uncontrollably.

"Is there anything I can do?" The words spoken, she knew she was potentially opening a Pandora's Box.

"Mommy, I just can't handle all of this by myself. Daddy needs me, but I know I'm just not up to it. Daddy asked me not to bother you with this, but I just can't handle it alone. I'm not even sure I can handle it with your help," confessed the girl.

"Did the doctor suggest anything?"

"He said we could try to find a hospice for Daddy to stay in or let him stay at home with supervision." Marion closed her eyes and took a deep breath. Starting with the day that she was relieved of her job back in February, responsibility had been a fourteen-letter word and nothing else to her. Now, it was on the brink of reclaiming its old friend, Marion Bell.

"Darling, if you can hang on another couple of days, I'll be down to help you out with your father. I'll leave for Connecticut on Tuesday or Wednesday morning, first thing. Tell your dad it will not be an imposition, okay honey?"

"Thank you, Mommy," replied Mia.

The phone call with her daughter took something out of Marion but it was not without its high points. For one thing, mother and daughter had not been able to communicate with this level of frankness in some time. In addition, Mia had not addressed her mother as 'mommy' in close to ten years. For this reason, Marion was able to take away something positive from the call even though the overriding message was very negative. She was in the act of returning to her comfortable chair in front of the television when Jimmy descended the stairs and walked half consciously toward the kitchen for his morning coffee.

"I know a certain young stud who isn't going to know what hit him when he has to leave the utopia that is Wells Beach and has to go back to the real world," she called out to the kitchen.

"I heard something about a stud my fine lady but nothing else," he hollered back. A few seconds passed and the twenty-two-year old appeared in the doorway to the living room with his coffee cup pressed against his lips.

"I was beginning to think that my tired old self had left you for dead up there. What's going to happen when you trade me in for a newer model? My God, if she's under thirty-five you're liable to be concluding a night of sex with an ambulance ride," she joked. Jimmy slowly closed his eyes, a pained expression spread across his face.

"Can we talk about anything but the end of summer," he muttered then collapsed onto the couch. "Who was that you were talking with on the phone?" he asked.

"Mia. I'm afraid her father has been diagnosed with something quite serious. She's asked me to come down and help out and I've agreed."

"Yeah, I was kind of afraid of that," blurted out Jimmy. His words caused her to look away from the television and train her eyes on him.

"What's that? You knew her father was having some health issues?" Her question produced a visible, nervous reaction from him.

"Yeah. I think you had mentioned something about it to me." Marion knitted her brow.

"I don't think so," she responded and intensified her stare across the room.

"Then maybe Mia could have mentioned something about it to me. We've talked on the phone a couple of times since her visit," he confessed. His words caused her to straighten up in her chair.

"Wow, that's the first I've heard about this. Is there anything else going on that I should be aware of?"

"There's nothing going on, Marion. We've just kept in touch since that weekend she spent up here," he added. She shot him another curious look before attempting to return her attention to the television. *What the hell is this? He's sitting over there looking as guilty as hell while attempting to look blasé about this whole matter. Are those two interested in each other and what if they are? Am I unwittingly in the middle of a Mrs. Robinson affair here?*

"I've already told Mia that I'll be down right after Labor Day. The plan is for me to drive back to Connecticut on Tuesday morning. At this point, I'm not completely sure where I'll be staying. My guess is it will be at my old house, but my ex could have a problem with that. If he does then I guess I may have to just stay with your parents," announced Marion. Her words caused Jimmy's eyes to open wide. It brought on a burst of laughter from her. "Don't have a heart attack, Jimmy. I was only kidding." He let out a long, relieved sigh.

"How long do you think you'll be staying with Mia and Mr. Bell?"

"My best guess is that I'll be there until my ex-husband passes. He has cancer and it sounds like it's in an advanced stage," she answered. "That means my dear, dear boy, tonight and tomorrow night will doubtlessly be our last together. So, with that in mind, I think we should make the most of them. It reminds me of a song from my youth. I apologize in advance for my voice. She cleared her throat and immediately broke into song.

> *It was a good time, it was the best time,*
>
> *It was a party just to be near you.*

She looked up and saw he had turned quite serious, an expression of sadness and, maybe, regret having taken hold of him.

"I would keep going but I can see you're the sentimental type. Maybe that's why I cared for you so much, that sensitivity. Trust me, lover, the rest of the lyrics would probably tear both of us apart. Anyway, given that we've never even discussed any other song as far as I can remember, *It Was a Good Time* will have to be our song from this day forward," she declared.

"But I don't even know it," exclaimed Jimmy. "How can it be our song if I don't even know half the lyrics?"

"Dearest, just go on-line and look it up. It's from a movie. Eydie Gorme sang the version I'm familiar with," she added. "Now, I think we ought to tie a bow around the remainder of this weekend. We always knew this time had to come and knew just about when after your folks came up to see you. Let's make the best of it. I think it's wise to avoid any public appearances together anywhere around Wells. The renters next door probably know your parents and the last thing we need to do is run into them at Billy's Chowder House or the Maine Diner. No, we'll go all the way to Portsmouth and find a nice, relaxed place where we can nurse a couple of drinks and have the meal of our lives. On Monday morning we'll have a contest of some kind to determine who must roll out of bed early and drive up to Congdon's. Mother of God, I've craved those donuts all summer! I'm five pounds under my ideal weight so it's time to bust loose. It's the weekend of pleasure. Plenty of time in the sack and sweet pastry to boot. What do you say?"

"You buy, I'll fly," volunteered Jimmy in the next breath. "But, I'm a little short for the drinks and dinner segment of the weekend," he admitted sheepishly. His admission brought a spurt of laughter from Marion.

"Lover boy, it's on me," said Marion. "It will help me beat back the guilt I've been feeling lately. Sometimes I feel like one of those she devils in the old horror movies, the ones that suck the youth out of their young lovers so they can remain young looking. Maybe I don't have the youthful looks to show for it but, I swear, you've made me feel oh so youthful this summer," she confessed.

"Marnie, you look great for your age and you know it."

"Yes…for my age. The devil's in the details and the detail is my age. Sweet Jesus, I'll be half a century old in just over two years. They demolish buildings that are younger than me."

Marion and Jimmy left for Portsmouth at shortly after two o'clock. On arrival, they walked the sidewalks of the historical city peeking in shop windows and commenting on any curious or bizarre items for sale. *It's interesting. Two months ago, I would have been self-conscious about being out in public with Jimmy and showing even the slightest bit of affection. Now, it seems like the most natural thing in the world. I'm not sure if that's a good or a bad thing.* Exploring even the narrowest of streets, they eventually followed an alleyway to a book shop beneath ground level where Marion bought Jimmy a coffee table book dedicated to images from the 1970s.

"This is to remember me by. The decade when I was in my prime. Back when music was great, maybe not as great as the sixties but still great. Jimmy, I wish you could have known me back then," she lamented.

"I don't know. Even knowing you today is pretty, damn special," he confessed. They eventually meandered upon a restaurant close to the harbor with a visually impressive bar. It was two and one-half hours between the time spent to seat themselves at the bar and when they cleared the front door of the establishment following their dinner. Jimmy had nursed a single martini over the course of their drinks and meal in Portsmouth but not Marion who polished off four Bloody Marys. Therefore, it surprised neither of them when it was she who left the restaurant on slightly unsteady legs. By mutual decision, Jimmy climbed behind the wheel for the ride back to Wells Beach. "I'm warning you, Marnie. If you think by passing out back at the house you'll be avoiding making love then you've learned nothing of me over the summer," he warned. She broke out laughing, her reaction having more to do with her state of inebriation than his amorous threat.

Marion curled her body sideways until she was looking directly at Jimmy across the front seat. She reached out and fiddled with the collar of his shirt. He observed that his lover was further under the influence of alcohol at this moment than, at any time, over the course of the spring and summer.

"How am I ever going to say goodbye to you?" she lamented. He reached across to her, placing the palm of his hand on her cheek. She moved her head up and down affectionately. Jimmy remained silent for the next few seconds before picking up on an apparent change of mood on her part. Glancing over, she appeared to be weeping.

"What's this? Why the tears?"

"It's just now hitting me that my life is about to change from something just this side of heaven to a living hell," she exclaimed. "For the sake of my daughter and no one else, I have volunteered to sit by and wait on the man who tossed me aside for another woman less than a year ago. Pray that you never have to experience anything like that. The feeling of betrayal and rejection leaves a scar."

"Marnie, if anyone has bounced back from that ordeal, you have," he added.

"My sweet boy, so much of the credit for that goes to you. Your attention propped me up more than you can ever realize," she confessed. *Oh God, I'm drunk and I'm spilling my guts. They say that in wine there is truth and, at this moment, I'm living testimony to it. Maybe this is good, leaving nothing unsaid.*

"You know, before all of this started up, I was about to warn you that even passing out on me back at the house is not going to save you. I plan on making passionate love to you whether you're awake or passed out. I think the latter could be against the law, but I don't give a rat's ass," he declared.

"Laws are made to be broken," said Marion loudly through moderately slurred speech. He reached down and squeezed her thigh just above the knee. She closed her eyes and allowed her head to slump backwards onto the vehicle headrest.

"May I ask a big favor of you, Jimmy?"

"Yes. The answer is yes," he replied instantaneously.

"Don't be so quick to agree. You haven't heard what I'm going to ask for. I've been drinking. It could be anything."

"No, you're right. I can't be agreeing to anything just because it's coming from you. You could be about to ask me to make love to a man or put a live spider in my mouth," he reasoned.

"No Jimmy, it's nothing like that. Tonight, back at the house and up in the bedroom, would you allow me to restrain you? You know, tie you down? The thought of having you totally under my control is getting me all hot and bothered. I mean, I've gone my whole life hearing about all sorts of kinky things and never have I once tried any of it. This could be my last chance and who better with than my young stud?"

"Your last chance? Let's be honest here. If word ever got out that Marion Bell, fortyish femme fatale with a body to die for, was in search of a man to restrain in her bedroom, there would be a line out the front door of the house and extending a quarter-of-a-mile up Atlantic Avenue," he predicted. Her eyes still closed, a smile broke across Marion's face.

"You're right. Men are all fools. They'll agree to most anything to get a woman into bed."

"Yes, we are."

"So, it's decided. Jimmy Sullivan…stripped naked and lying bound and gagged on my bed," said Marion.

"Whoa, what's this gagged thing? Why do I have to be gagged?"

"Because you have to be totally and absolutely helpless. No yelling for help if I should come up with something truly wild and erotic," she explained. "And, besides, you have to sing for your supper. I paid for drinks and dinner," she reminded him.

"So, there were strings attached to this night out."

"You sound like you've never done anything like this before."

"I haven't!" exclaimed Jimmy.

"My lover, just put your trust in me. You have to know that I would never hurt you," purred Marion. He glanced across the cab of the car and nodded in the affirmative.

Chapter 13

Marion's sexual escapade in restraint took the two lovers well into the wee hours of the morning. Marion satisfied a reservoir of passionate urges on this night, not knowing when the next opportunity for intense pleasure might arrive. For Jimmy, he came away with a heightened awareness of true, sexual vulnerability and the knowledge that any further adventures in this tenuous playground must be carried out in the company of a trustworthy partner, a partner akin to Marion Bell. Wet with perspiration, Marion and Jimmy sat half-dressed in the living room in the early morning hours of Labor Day, 2002. He was uncharacteristically subdued.

"Was it what you expected?" she asked, breaking nearly a minute of silence.

"It was more, a lot more. I had a hunch it would take me into that whole pleasure/pain thing, but it was even more intense than I anticipated. Marnie, you didn't hold back. In the back of my head I knew I could trust you, but I started imagining how I would feel if it had been someone else in control. It's a little scary." She smiled and inched closer to him on the couch.

"Yes, you would have to be very careful. What I kept running over and over in my head is how this would be the last time in my life I would ever get my hands on such a young, sacrificial lamb," she joked. He leaned sideways and kissed her on the crown of her head.

"I've been putting off telling you something, but our time together is growing short," he confessed in a deeply serious tone. She stared into his eyes. "Marnie, I don't want us to return to Connecticut with this hanging out there. There should be no secrets between us."

"I agree completely," she answered.

"You've already surmised that Mia and I are closer than either of us let on to you," he stated. "The last thing in the world I want to see happen is for you to learn something about us from a third party." Marion straightened up on the couch and pulled back slightly from him. "I didn't say anything at the time but that week she came to visit here made an impression on me. Now, it's more than the family resemblance between the two of you but I'm sure that had something to do with it. From day one I could see a lot of you in her. Even after she went back home we kept in touch. I told you we talked a few times but that was a lie. We spoke on the phone almost every day. Naturally, I didn't tell her about you and me," he added.

"Thank heavens for small miracles," she interrupted.

"To this day, Mia doesn't know a thing about you and me and I sincerely doubt she even suspects anything. Marnie, it will stay that way as long as that's what you want," he promised.

"I want it that way," she answered curtly. He fidgeted in place, telling Marion his confession was not over.

"Everything I've told you up until now was, technically, not a lie. I just omitted something," he reasoned.

"It was a lie of omission," she injected. He nodded in agreement.

"What clearly was a lie was the story I told you a few weekends ago. That weekend I told you I was going home to attend the wedding of a high school friend was really a trip back to Connecticut to spend with Mia. There is no sugar coating that, it was a lie. Mia wanted it kept a secret even without the knowledge of our relationship," admitted Jimmy. Marion glared at him long and hard before closing her eyes and resting her head on the back of the couch.

"Was there sex?" she asked.

"Yes." She closed her fist and struck him on the shoulder.

"You couldn't even wait until we were no more," she bristled, anger and disappointment evident in her tone.

"I'll leave right now if that's what you want," he muttered.

"No, the last thing I need is to have you fall asleep at the wheel and kill yourself and maybe even someone else. You can sleep in one of the other bedrooms. But, I want you packed and gone by tomorrow afternoon," she ordered. He nodded his head in acceptance. "Oh, and there is one more thing I insist on," she stated. "I want your word that you take the knowledge of what happened between you and me to the grave. Is that understood?"

"Mrs. Bell, I will tell no one what happened, particularly Mia and my parents. That means the secret lies with only the two of us because I haven't mentioned it to a soul." *He chose his words carefully. He called me, Mrs. Bell. We both know this insane affair is over.*

Marion spent a restless night and morning alone in her bed. Still stunned by Jimmy's revelation, she lay in bed until the sound of activity in the kitchen brought her totally to her senses. Responding to the slamming of a car's trunk, she scurried out of bed and wrapped herself in a bathrobe. Unable to locate her slippers, she descended the stairwell barefoot and went in search of Jimmy. He was nowhere to be found on the first floor of the house. Scurrying to the front door, she spied his vehicle parked at the far end of the driveway. He was sitting motionless behind the wheel. *Just let it be. Everything's been said. There are no soft landings at the end of something like this.* Following a moment's hesitation, she turned and walked back into the kitchen. The coffee maker's light was on and the carafe was half full. Strolling halfway across the room, she plucked a cup from the cupboard and filled it.

Marion claimed a chair at the table and drew in her first sip of coffee. Glancing up at the clock, she saw that it was a few minutes shy of noontime. A few moments passed and then came the sound of Jimmy's car engine coming to life. She turned toward the road and watched the vehicle turn out of the driveway and head southward. Jimmy Sullivan's summer was over, she thought. Her mind went back to her conversation in the wee hours of the morning. *I know I can trust him to keep his word on the matter of the affair. He would have nothing to gain by divulging anything. I'm sorry it had to end this way, but it was important that everything was brought out into the open now and not later.* She rose to her feet and reviewed what might be on hand for a late breakfast. She was disappointed to find only some low-calorie cereal and wheat bread for toast. She let out a moan of disgust and shuffled into the living room. A disheveled blanket lay spread across the couch where Jimmy had made his confession a few hours earlier. The sight of it depressed her. She stepped across the room and settled into her favorite chair. She drew in a deep breath and took another sip of coffee. She glanced in the direction of the darkened television to the sound of an opening door. Turning toward the hallway, she saw Jimmy Sullivan appear in the doorway to the room. He appeared anxious.

"I couldn't just leave without saying goodbye," he stated almost apologetically. She placed her coffee cup on a nearby table and walked in his direction. Wrapping her arms around him, she rested her head on his chest.

"You will always be special...so very special to me," she confessed and breathed into the fabric of his shirt.

"Marnie, I will always feel an affection for you that I don't think I will ever feel for anyone else. You may not know it, but you rebuilt me, my ego and self-confidence, I mean," he confided.

"And you, Jimmy Sullivan, gave me my *Summer of 42* and *Last Tango in Paris* right here within the walls of this house," confessed Marion. "Please forgive me for my movie references, particularly given that they both pre-dated you by at least ten years. He peppered the crown of her head with kisses before lifting her chin with the tips of his fingers and kissing her passionately on the mouth. The kiss lingered for an extended moment before they separated. They stood staring at each other before Marion lifted her fingers to her lips and gestured him to be on his way. He responded with a tender smile, turned and walked from this magnificent chapter of Marion Bell's life.

Chapter 14

Marion spent Labor Day afternoon packing for her trip back to Connecticut and reliving many of the high points of the summer of 2002. She had learned from Mia that doctors familiar with Monty's case gave him three to six months to live. She set her mind on staying for the duration of his illness unless asked not to stay. She saw little chance of being sent away. She packed mostly work and casual clothes in addition to a conservative, black dress and shoes. Eventually her mind wandered away from the gloomy matters awaiting her in Connecticut and back to subjects of a more positive nature. *I'm so glad Jimmy couldn't leave without making things right between us. It would have been terrible having that dark cloud hanging over the entire summer. God, what a remarkable kid. There's no completely forgiving his antics with Mia and the lies that came after but he's human like everyone else. My Lord, what an incredible secret the two of us will harbor from this day until our graves, particularly if something really develops between him and Mia. In any event, given his relationship with my daughter and the proximity of the Sullivan house to mine, I think it's safe to say that Jimmy Sullivan will remain, to some extent, in my life well into the future.*

By six o'clock Marion's luggage was packed and resting in the front hallway. In addition, all spoilable foods had been consumed or discarded giving the kitchen the look of a household mired in the great depression. Standing in the middle of the living room, she glanced eastward and out to sea. She was struck by the thought of having to live away from the ocean for the next few months. She remembered the words of the nuns back in grade school. "Offer it up as penance for the sins of your past life," they would preach. *Now I have something to have penance for*, she thought. She turned and caught sight of herself in the mirror. In her tight jeans and form-fitting tee shirt, she was not the slightly frumpy, forty-seven-year old that rolled up to the house less than four months earlier. She walked to the porch door and took in the shoreline fifty feet beyond her porch. It looked inviting.

Marion discarded her sandals and made the walk down to the water's edge. The sun was descending slowly and cast her shadow out over the foaming surf. The ocean smelled wonderful and fresh on this evening. It was dinnertime but there were still walkers strolling by the edge of the Atlantic, no doubt grasping at the final few hours of the prime, vacation season. Inching forward, her toes reached the cold sea water. This was goodbye to her beloved beach, at least for the time being, she thought. If the doctors were correct, she would not return to her beach house until winter. Peering out over the blue water to the horizon, she felt small. *Lord, we haven't spoken for a while, a good long while. I may have even cursed you out last year when you seemed to be throwing heaven and earth at me. You must admit, I've had it rough lately up until this summer and now even that's behind me. Oh, by the way, thank you for sending me Jimmy. I promise it'll never happen again, but I don't regret a second of my time with him.*

"Beautiful time of the day," called out a woman strolling a few feet away. She and her husband smiled and continued past Marion, not waiting on a response. Marion acknowledged the comment with a smile. It was wasted on the back of their heads. The encounter came as a reminder of her status, single and unattached. She shrugged off the interruption and looked back out to sea.

Lord, it's me again. I guess what I'm doing here is saying that I'm back on solid ground, emotionally that is. As you know, I leave tomorrow to care for my ex-husband. There are a thousand other things I'd rather be doing but, for some unknown reason, I volunteered so here I am. I know my love for my daughter certainly had something to do with my decision and maybe in a very small way I don't want Monty suffering or being alone. But, in the end, it's the right thing to do. It's what You would have done. So, keep it in mind down the road. I think back to what I felt like in April and May, the loneliness I mean. I'm no spring chicken. I'll be forty-eight in a little over a month. Please, don't be afraid to throw me a bone. I'm not asking for another Jimmy Sullivan. Just throw me a bone.

Marion turned and began the half mile walk to the jetty. Checking her watch, she saw there was at least another hour of sunlight. Walking northward, she turned inland and viewed the remains of sand dunes buffering the beach cottages at the far end of Atlantic Avenue from the surging Atlantic Ocean. She always preferred walking at this end of the beach where there were fewer pebbles to aggravate a good, barefoot walk. Approaching the jetty, she looked up and remembered her first genuine encounter with Jimmy. *I can't believe how immature he was that day. I thought there was something wrong with him mentally. The way he would keep brushing against me and placing his hands on my shoulders. A part of me wanted to distance myself from him but only a part of me. Clearly, the other part of me won out.* She turned from the elevated walkway of granite boulders and retraced her footsteps in the direction of the house.

Marion's half mile walk back to the house was taken up with thoughts of Monty and what physical condition she would find him in the next day. The sun had fallen low in the sky, barely peaking above the outline of structures and trees lining Route 1 a mile to the west. Reaching the expanse of beach adjacent to her house, she turned from the foaming surf and began the short walk to her back door.

"Don't tell me you're one of those rich folks who own oceanfront property? It's a hike to either parking lot so you have to be," continued a male voice from behind. She whirled around and focused her eyes on a stranger sporting a white moustache and silver hair.

"That would be my business. Do I even know you?" challenged Marion behind a stare that outwardly unsettled the man. He quickly attempted to recover.

"You do in a manner of speaking. We spoke in the supermarket a month or two ago. I was the Mandarin oranges guy," he explained.

"What the hell are you talking about? Are you on medication?" She watched as the bravado on display only moments earlier seem to ooze out of the stranger's body. He grew apologetic.

"I spoke to you in the IGA about whether to buy the name brand or the store brand of products. You happened to be holding a can of Mandarin oranges at the time," he explained. Her aggravated stare transformed into a slight smile.

"You have a good memory," she replied. The man let his head drop in an apologetic manner.

"It's just that you were walking quite a way at the edge of the ocean and then turned abruptly toward the houses. I wanted to initiate a conversation and that stupid comment somehow came to mind," he muttered.

"How do you know I've been walking a long way? Have you been stalking me?" she asked accusingly. She was playing with her prey at this point.

"No, I was just following you out of curiosity."

"To what end, Mandarin orange man?" The man laughed and was relieved to see the smile on his tormentor's face.

"Just to see where you lived and maybe strike up a conversation with you," he explained.

"To see where I live. In other words, to stalk me." The stranger shook his head no. She resumed walking only to have the man block her path. He reached out a hand.

"My name is Gary Tillotson," he announced and waited on her response. She clutched his hand.

"Nice to know you, Gary Tillotson," she answered before stepping around him and continuing toward the house. *I'm completely in control here. I think I'll make him suffer just a little bit longer.*

"And your name?" he asked apprehensively. She whirled around and stared confidently into his eyes.

"Marnie," she replied.

"Marnie what?" She delayed her response for a few moments.

"Tell me, Mandarin orange man, what comes to mind when you hear the name, Marnie?" There was no hesitation in the man's response.

"I think of the Hitchcock movie with Tippi Hedren," he answered. Marion's face brightened.

"Right answer," she responded. Tillotson grew emboldened by her reaction.

"Listen…Marnie, if your young stud is still in the picture, I think I have a pretty good idea what your answer to my question will be…but here goes. Would you ever consider joining me for a cup of coffee or a dinner or anything? Something to let us get to know each other a little more."

"My young stud and I have amicably parted ways and the answer to your question is a definite maybe."

"When?"

"I'm afraid my house will go dark for a few months, but I will be back. So, if you're serious, you only need to watch for my return. You know where I live," said Marion while stepping up onto her porch.

"I'll watch for the lights in your house to return. I promise, I'll pass by every night until I see that you've returned." She turned back to him and flashed a warm smile.

"See that you do, Mandarin orange man. See that you do."

Little Henrietta

The automobile rolled methodically onto the driveway and deliberately made its way toward the Bruckner House, the sound of fallen leaves crunching between rubber and cobblestone as it advanced. Fifty feet from the roadway, the vehicle came to a stop and down rolled the driver's window. From inside the oversized car a round, male face stared up at the early nineteenth century structure. The weathered, darkened brown colonial home represented his life's work or at least the last two and a half years of it and he looked upon it with a certain awe. Less than an hour earlier, Jonathan Turley acquired the stately residence from the Portland bank that had financed its purchase from the previous owner only months before the real estate collapse of 1988.

Turley, his eyes lovingly glued to the exterior of his acquisition, turned off the auto's engine and awkwardly rotated his body out of the driver's seat. It certainly was a massive house for a single man, he thought. Gazing over his shoulder, he was taken with the length of the driveway back to Elm Street. Although hunched within one of Kennebunkport, Maine's most densely populated neighborhoods, the Bruckner House somehow managed to remain practically invisible to the casual pedestrian strolling anywhere in the immediate neighborhood.

Jonathan Turley, this tale's main character, was considered a successful man in the community but with no shortage of critics. It was said of him that he could fit his lifetime of friendships into a booth at the Maine Diner while his enemies list would face standing room only conditions at a gathering at Fenway Park. He was, for certain, not a religious man. Turley fervently believed that charity began at home and, therefore, made a point of living alone.

Climbing the two granite steps that addressed the building's front door, he pulled the ring of five keys from his pocket and manipulated the lock. A moment later the heavy door swung in and exposed a carpeted hallway and unassuming stairwell. Turley stepped inside and closed the door behind him. No use in letting any cold, October air into his house, he reasoned. Turning right, he made his way into the living room, already his favorite spot in the house. This room showcased two book cases set into an interior wall that framed a marble fireplace. In addition, the room was the beneficiary of much natural light thanks to the arch of windows forming a solarium on the east end of the residence. This living room was appointed with Victorian furniture and donned individual portraits of a man and a woman, no doubt former occupants of the residence. The new owner tossed his jacket down onto a chair by the doorway and set out to raise a fire.

It was a satisfied Jonathan Turley who fell back onto the living room couch after the first evening meal in his new home. Settling for a dinner of cold cut sandwiches and potato salad, he settled in for a quiet evening of reading and paperwork. The bulk of the afternoon had been spent moving in clothing and some personal effects from his Kennebunk apartment. With cable installation still days away, his television sat dark against the far wall. Early into the evening he paused and let the exhilaration of the moment wash over him. He had all but stolen the house from the bank, he thought. He chuckled out loud within the quiet walls of the room at the thought of the recent call from Al Sneed, the Portland loan officer who had denied him the property on three previous occasions. It was a different Mr. Sneed on this last occasion. It was the 'yes Mr. Turley' and 'no Mr. Turley' Sneed in their most recent discussions. So, thanks to his patience and the cash realized from his mother's life insurance policy, he had stolen the grand, old house for half of its worth. On a whim, the forty-eight-year-old bachelor rose from the couch and set out on a tour of the first and second floors. With a bottle of beer in hand, he crossed the downstairs hallway and pushed open the door to the spacious sitting room. This floor space was immense and filled him with pride. Spreading the width of the building, the room was dominated by a large fireplace on its interior wall and showcased elevated windows across the three, exterior walls in addition to the best collection of furniture in the entire house. Immediately, his eyes locked on a large painting of a Madonna figure above the fireplace. Crossing the room, he pulled the work of art from the wall and leaned it, upside down, by the doorway, making a mental note to find a suitable place for the religious painting in an outbuilding. Across the hallway and adjacent to the living room was a forgettable dining room behind which stood the kitchen. Turley spent little to no time in these last two rooms, content to review them in greater detail the following day.

After shutting the doors to the large, front room, he climbed the stairs to the second floor. It was the second floor that had, most surely, dampened the interest of some prospective buyers during previous tours of the property. He remembered that on two separate occasions the individual conducting the tour had disclosed some dark details involving two of the bedrooms upstairs. Prospective buyers had learned that the large, sprawling master bedroom had not been used for its primary purpose since just before World War II when the matriarch of the family passed away unexpectedly. Also offered for public consumption was the fact that the small bedroom at the rear of the house had long been referred to as the 'death' room because of its history as the room assigned to gravely ill members of the household in their last months among the living. For these reasons, Jonathan had chosen the third bedroom as his own. It was a pleasant room and came with a solarium corner and functioning fireplace.

Turley retired to bed before ten o'clock on his first night at the Bruckner

House. He enjoyed a quiet, uninterrupted sleep and rose for work at sunrise the following morning.

The offices of Turley & Associates, LLC were small and less than inspiring. Located at the rear of a colorless building in nearby Wells, the office space covered a little over four hundred square feet and was manned by one fulltime and one part-time employee. As for Turley's associates, they existed in his company's letterhead and nowhere else, created exclusively for image. Jonathan Turley was an investment advisor and made a reasonably good living servicing middle class families and individuals in York County, Maine. He spent the better part of the morning after his purchase enthusiastically describing his new residence to April Grant, his nineteen-year-old secretary, office manager and office wife. Recruited for the job directly out of high school at age seventeen, April had met Turley's simple hiring profile: She was reasonably attractive, somewhat timid and lacked a boyfriend.

Jonathan's exuberance over the new house propelled him to his residence early on this Thursday afternoon. On the drive home to Kennebunkport, he began devising a plan to lure April over to the house. Most women love decorating and she was probably no exception to the rule, he thought. He would court her advice even if he had no intention of following it. It was a good plan, he thought, while traversing the narrow streets in town. The Bruckner House would certainly appeal to any materialistic urges harbored within her.

The final leg of his commute home brought him through Dock Square. The high-end gift shops and general sophistication of the downtown streets reinforced his present state of excitement. He perceived heightened social status with his move from Kennebunk. His car did a half circle around the town center and within sixty seconds he was parked outside the Bruckner House. The muted silence from within the house amplified the sound of the front door as the new owner stepped inside. Turley had already decided to explore the second and third floors in more detail on this afternoon. Following a change of clothing, he exited his bedroom and stepped to the base of the flight of stairs leading up to the attic rooms. He distinctly remembered his reaction to the attic area on the first of his auction tours. At the time, he remembered being pleasantly surprised to see individual rooms and not a single expanse of floor space on the uppermost floor of the mansion. Moving deliberately up the steps toward the closed door above him, halfway to the attic, he thought he heard a female voice from the floor above. The adult voice sounded both muffled and strangely distant. There was no one else in house, he thought. He rationalized that somehow the female's voice had to be drifting over from a neighboring residence. It was the only logical explanation. Stopping in mid step, he paused while the woman's voice continued unabated. Somewhat shaken, he cautiously moved upward until the attic doorknob was within his grasp. He turned the knob. The metallic sounding rotation of the doorknob caused the unexplainable voice to stop in mid syllable. A shutter of fear pierced the pit of his stomach.

"What the hell is going on?" he whispered to himself. Following only a moment's hesitation, he turned and retreated down the flight of stairs to the second floor. He needed time to make sense of his circumstances.

In the twenty-four hours since the closing on the property, Turley had already grown fond of the extensive sitting room on the first floor. For this reason, he dragged a small work table from a storage room at the back of the house into one corner directly in front of a comfortable Victorian chair. Collapsing onto the chair, he looked across the better than three hundred square feet of living area and substantial fireplace at the back wall. It was a room that conjured up the image of social gatherings from another era and the reverberation of spirited conversation, he thought. Eventually, his mind drifted back to the incident on the third floor. He was sure he had heard a woman's voice from behind the door and it was no coincidence that her words had ceased the moment he had turned the doorknob. He had never believed in ghosts and generally mocked anyone who professed they did. However, the strange encounter with something earlier in the day at the attic door gave him pause to reconsider his position.

By the time the autumn sun had descended on the southern coast of Maine, Jonathan had both the living and sitting room fireplaces ablaze at the Bruckner House. In his work corner of the sprawling sitting room, workpapers were strewn across the table. He had already taken the time to assemble some of his most valued possessions in the room. Of note was one of his most prized possessions; an eight-inch-long hunting knife once owned by Hannibal Hamlin, a Maine native and Abraham Lincoln's first vice-president. Turley already proudly kept it in plain sight at the corner of his cluttered table. It was shortly after eight o'clock when his mind emerged from a short stack of client's financial records and, again, flashed back to the inexplicable woman's voice at the top of the stairs. The more he ran the incident over in his head, the more he was convinced there was a spirit domiciled on the third floor of his house. He momentarily considered contacting a priest and asking to have the house blessed before immediately dismissing the idea. He had long hated Catholicism or, for that matter, anything Christian. No, there had to be a more scientific way of dealing with the problem, he reasoned. He craved some form of diversion but cable service was still a day away and television reception with a set of rabbit ears was pitiful. He visited the kitchen and brought two cans of Budweiser back to his table. He decided to work until he could no longer remain awake.

The sitting room was dressed only in the flickering light from the fireplace's smoldering embers when Turley blinked open his eyes and realized he had dozed off some time earlier. He vaguely remembered turning off the overhead lamp for a brief nap at approximately ten o'clock. Glancing around the room, the businessman was hard pressed to distinguish any of the surrounding furniture in the muted light. It was just before raising himself to his feet that he detected movement in the doorway across the room. Straining his eyes, he watched as a largely indiscernible object came in his direction, its movement best described as gliding. The hair on the back of his neck stood on end as his body locked up in fear. It moved in absolute silence until its form became somewhat visible in the dying light from the fire. It was a child, a young girl of no more than five of six years. She was dressed in a flannel nightgown that dropped down to just above her ankles and appeared to be a character straight out of a Louisa May Alcott novel. The apparition stared up at him through dark eyes, eyes that seemed to cry out for help. She was a beautiful little creature, he thought.

"I can't find my mommy. I can't find her anywhere," she declared pitifully. Jonathan peered down on the child and knew instinctively she was not from the here and now. He stared wide-eyed, paralyzed in fear yet curious about the beautiful, little girl standing before him. The spirit began to whimper and reached out for him. She established contact with his hand before he could pull it away. He was amazed to find that she was comprised of solid mass, her hand and fingers cool but not cold to the touch. "Please help me find my mommy," she implored. An instant later she turned back toward the door as if roused by someone or something. She shot Turley a final glance over her shoulder and moved toward the far doorway. Again, her feet made no sound on the floorboards. Reaching the hall, she vanished and Turley was left alone on the first floor of the house.

Ten minutes after the disappearance of the spirit of the young girl, Jonathan gathered up his workpapers and retired for the evening. Stepping out into the kitchen, he plucked a can of beer from his refrigerator and quietly moved up the stairwell to his bedroom. His rational side told him that his memory of the visit from the little girl was only the result of an overworked mind.

Chapter 2

Jonathan glanced to his nightstand and focused on the face of the alarm clock. It was a few minutes after three o'clock. He had been lying awake and mentally replaying the events of this night over and over in his head. He was having a difficult time coming to grips with the reality of what had transpired: the beautiful child that he had encountered was not from the world of the living, he repeated to himself. He had tried closing his eyes to induce sleep, but the image of the child's face continued to haunt him. Suddenly, the absolute stillness within the building was broken by the cry of a woman's voice from the attic rooms above. His nerves shattered, he jumped from the bed and hurriedly threw on his clothes. He exited the house with overcoat and shoes in hand and hurried up the driveway to the relative safety of the road. Badly shaken by the activity from within the house, he walked in the direction of lights and storefronts, Dock Square. The dark exteriors of Alisson's Restaurant and the Colonial Pharmacy greeted him on arrival. With his mind only now beginning to clear, he questioned his decision to walk to the center of town and not employ his automobile. After roaming the sidewalks and alleyways of the downtown area for nearly half an hour, he set out on foot for the open ocean. Two hours later, he watched the sun rise from beyond the watery horizon from a roadside bench between the Atlantic Ocean and the Colony Hotel.

By the time Turley returned to the Bruckner House, he had reasonably conquered his shock from the night before. There was no denying his mental state was registering somewhere between flustered and petrified on the matter of the female presence in the attic. However, it was quite the contrary regarding the young girl who had addressed him in the sitting room the evening before. Whether owing to her tender years or striking beauty, he harbored no resentment to sharing his newly acquired home with her, at least partly because he felt no physical threat associated with her presence.

It was the middle of the afternoon when the cable man arrived at the Bruckner House and wired the residence for television service. Turley saw this as a welcome return to the twentieth century from what felt like a tour of Victorian times. The arrival of the sound and imagery of one hundred channels came as a distraction from the thoughts of unnatural voices and visits from the non-living. For the next few days and nights he lived in constant fear of the female specter residing in the uppermost rooms of his house. However, for the next week he spent his evenings in the relative calm of a quiet house.

At the office, April Grant finally agreed to visit the Bruckner House and, it was agreed, she would do so on the last Saturday of October. With a few days in hand, Turley went room to room, cleaning, dusting, polishing and, in general, setting out to make his two hundred-year-old home as appealing as possible to his young secretary. First impressions are important, he reminded himself, as he moved from chore to chore in anticipation of April's visit. It was a physically exhausted Jonathan Turley who sat spread out in front of his television on a Tuesday night. He flicked off the tv and tried to muster the energy to rise to his feet and make the walk upstairs to the bedroom. The room had grown chilly, he thought, despite the flames still dancing within the marble fireplace. Sluggishly, he stood up and turned for the hallway. To his amazement, standing in the corner and heretofore out of sight, was the young girl from his prior visitation, her beautiful, dark eyes riveted on him. She moved in his direction, soundless, gliding footsteps bringing her to within a foot of his position. Wide-eyed, he stared hypnotically down on the girl. It was the same beautiful child that he had encountered a week earlier but something was different about her, he thought. He fell back onto his chair, never breaking eye contact. Still dressed in what he perceived to be nineteenth century sleeping attire, she crouched down onto the floor and stared up at him. Her hand touched his. Just as before, her flesh was cool to the touch. The girl's visible flesh, face, hands and feet, showed no sign of physical decomposition.

"My mother has gone and I cannot find her," she exclaimed sadly. Searching the young girl's face, he recognized the change in the child's appearance since their first encounter. The girl crouching before him was clearly older than the one he encountered a week earlier but it was the same child. The perfect, beautiful face staring up at him was that of an eight, perhaps even nine-year-old. He also estimated that she had added five or six inches in height.

"What's your name, young lady?" he asked. He spoke in just above a whisper for fear of scaring her.

"Henrietta," she answered but offered no surname. Turley reached down and affectionately stroked her hair. She came back with no response but offered no resistance to his show of familiarity. "Can you help me find my mommy?" she implored, her voice both hopeful and trusting.

"When did you last see her?" he asked. The question appeared to confuse the child. "What's your mommy's name?" he continued.

"Her name is Jane Porter," she answered. Turley's mind raced uncontrollably, the realization that he was interacting, both mentally and physically, with an entity from another dimension registering in his mind. "She was Jane Porter but then my daddy died and she married Mr. Wilson," explained the girl. Almost involuntarily, the man's right hand left the girl's hair and came to rest on her shoulder. "Please help me find my momma. I don't want to stay here with Mr. Wilson anymore," she exclaimed. The specter leaned forward and rested her head on Turley's lap, clearly soliciting his protection. The room grew silent while the middle-aged man undertook the futile task of remaining composed. Nothing in his forty-eight years on the planet had prepared him for this moment. He merely sat frozen in his chair. Then, the child's head abruptly rose from its resting place and turned back in the direction of the hall. An instant later, Henrietta was dashing from the room and out into the hallway. Turley scrambled to his feet and went in pursuit, but the child had disappeared by the time he reached the hall.

Jonathan Turley lay in bed on the night of his second visitation from Henrietta and attempted to process the events from the last week and a half. The psychological enormity of the developing relationship between himself and the child spirit was beyond anything with which he could come to grips. How does anyone process the unreal? To his knowledge, no one had ever verifiably communicated with the departed yet here he was asking questions of the dead and getting clear, definitive responses. Granted, she was a child and the depth to which he could potentially delve was limited, he reasoned. By all appearances, she was a troubled soul and he couldn't even begin to fathom any way he could be of assistance to her. However, he was fascinated by this experience and felt nothing in the way of a threat from the girl, psychologically or physically. He then began to consider the ways he might parlay this whole experience into a financial payoff. He had begun running the different possibilities of capturing little Henrietta on audio or video when he suddenly remembered the presence domiciled in the attic. Nearly a week had passed since he had heard anything from the top floor of the house and that suited him fine. He was reluctant to venture up to the attic alone, even during daylight hours, but he reasoned that he could face his fears in the company of another person. April would be visiting the house on Saturday. Why not treat her to the nickel tour and bring her upstairs? He vaguely remembered a stockpile of old furniture stored in the far room and this might be the opportunity to inspect it. By midnight his plans for the weekend were in place and Jonathan drifted off to sleep.

Chapter 3

A heavy, damp mist had settled on Maine's southern coast on the last Saturday of the month. It was shortly after eleven o'clock in the morning when Jonathan thought he heard a vehicle approaching the house and walked to the window to investigate. Pressing down on a living room Venetian blind, he caught sight of April Grant emerging from her Nissan Sentra. He was quick to notice that she was dressed more casually than was her custom in the office. He rushed to the front door and ushered the teenager inside with a flourish of transparently insincere bravado. After removing the teenager's jacket, the proud homeowner brought his guest directly to the dining room where lunch was already laid out on the spacious table. April had been told to arrive with an appetite and she had followed those instructions. The two shared a leisurely lunch of pea soup and ham and cheese sandwiches on homemade bread. The noontime meal was capped off with a plate of assorted fruit while the two lightheartedly discussed problems and challenges at the office.

The tour of the first and second stories of the house went smoothly with Jonathan providing just enough history of the building and furnishings to keep his young employee interested. April seemed particularly impressed when Turley explained the historical significance of the menacing knife left out in plain sight at his sitting room work station.

"I even have a certificate of authenticity," he bragged while waving the weapon around in front of him. Coincidentally, April had written a paper on Hannibal Hamlin in her junior year of high school and was able to comment quite intelligently on the former owner of the blade. When the two reached the second floor, Jonathan informed his young employee of his intention to explore the attic and encouraged her to let him know if she saw anything that struck her fancy. The offer seemed to bring a fresh enthusiasm to the girl and soon after they were climbing the stairs to the top of the house.

Turley turned the door handle and pushed inward. It was a grey, rainy day leaving only muted light to filter in from the small, octagonal windows at either end of the succession of rooms. A nervous energy sprang up in the man's stomach while his eyes darted left and right in search of anything out of the ordinary. What he saw was floor space draped in shadows and littered with objects largely associated with the past. The pair decided to make a pass through the rooms together before concentrating on any specific items of interest. The attic consisted of four successive rooms, each linked by a doorway. None of the doors had been left on its hinges. Each door had been left leaning against a nearby wall. Passing through the entirety of the top floor, the two explorers learned that the rooms at opposite ends of the attic contained the most items of inventory. On their initial inspection, Jonathan happened upon a single, working light bulb and employed it close by the stairwell landing. Eventually, his attention was drawn to a collection of furniture pieces stacked three high in the farthest room from the stairway while April decided to sift through a collection of household items two rooms away. The two separated and excitedly began their individual examinations, calling out to one another whenever an item struck their fancy. Fifteen minutes into the undertaking, Turley was congratulating himself for coming up with the idea of this antique hunt. It was evident to him that his young employee was enjoying herself. However, the tranquility of the moment came crashing in on him moments later when a female scream sliced through the stagnant air of the attic. The shriek came from April Grant two rooms away. Half buried in a stack of chairs, he scrambled over the furniture and ran toward his young employee. Reaching her, he found the young woman backed against the wall, her eyes wide open and scanning the room.

"Someone touched me," she cried out. "I felt a hand on my back," she added excitedly. Jonathan raced across the room and took hold of her.

"Are you sure you didn't just back into something?" he asked innocently, knowing he must not acknowledge the earlier problems with a spirit in the attic.

"I didn't back into anything," she insisted. "Whatever touched me had fingers. It was a hand, I tell you. I have to go," she exclaimed. She pushed her way past Jonathan and scurried toward the stairway. "You have a ghost in this house, Mr. Turley. Like it or not, you have a ghost." April rambled down the two flights of stairs with Jonathan in pursuit and went in search of her jacket. She found it in a small hallway adjacent to the dining room. She turned and was stopped in her tracks by her employer. Placing his hands on both of her shoulders, he locked eyes with her.

"I believe you," he declared in a soothing voice. "As crazy as it sounds, I still believe you." The young woman shook her head in disbelief, gesturing she was already questioning her own sanity. "I just hope you can act like nothing happened here. I'm afraid if you were to let on something strange happened at the house, people might start wagging their tongues and suggesting that I did something improper," he explained.

"Oh God, I know you didn't do anything wrong, Mr. Turley," responded April, placing a hand on his shoulder to emphasize her sincerity. He nodded to her in appreciation and escorted her to the door. The visit he had hoped to cultivate into a personal relationship had gone up in flames.

The days grew chillier as October colors yielded to the more austere month of November when most days take on the guise of a black and white movie. Over this period the Bruckner House had grown silent, absent all supernatural activity. Nearly two weeks passed from the day of April Grant's visit with nary a sound from the attic. Also absent was any indication of Henrietta's presence in the mansion. With the passage of time came the shortening of daylight hours. This was something Jonathan Turley could have done without.

On an unseasonably cold evening in the second week of November, Jonathan was busy with paperwork at his table in the house's spacious sitting room. On the far, interior wall the fireplace was ablaze sending both light and heat out to the far corners of the room. A floor lamp lit Turley's cluttered work station. He had been engrossed in detailed forms for the better part of four hours and lost all track of time. Glancing down at his watch, he was shocked to find the hour was rapidly approaching midnight. He drew in a deep breath and leaned against the back of his chair. Over the past two or three days, he had seriously begun to wonder if the spirit activity had played itself out. He proffered a theory that the visit upstairs to the attic by he and April had somehow defused the entity harbored in the darkness on the third floor above. He was about to flick off the floor lamp behind him when his eyes were alerted toward movement in the hallway. Something had passed the open door and disappeared into the living room. The activity had registered no sound.

Turley flicked off the sitting room lamp and stepped toward the hallway where a ceiling light provided illumination. Lingering in the doorway, he called out.

"Henrietta, is that you?" he asked into the dimly lit living room. There was no response. Reaching the edge of the room, he snapped on the overhead light. His eyes caught a momentary glimpse of a girl before she darted from her perch on the sofa and seemed to disappear behind an interior wall. "I'm so sorry, Henrietta. Did the light scare you?" There was no answer to his question nor did he expect one. He turned off the light and waited in near darkness for the specter to return.

Jonathan waited patiently in the silent living room for the next fifteen minutes in vain. Twice he called out to Henrietta to return but neither attempt was successful. He was just about to retire for the evening when there seemed to come an electrical sound of sorts from the general area of the fireplace. There his eyes picked up on the outline of the girl. She was seated on the hearth with her head balanced on her knees and her arms wrapped tightly around her legs. She was clothed in the same familiar dressing gown with only her bare feet left uncovered by the garment.

"The light hurts my eyes," she explained innocently. Her speech sounded more mature than he remembered.

"I don't want you feeling afraid or like you're not welcome when I'm here," answered Turley. Slowly, the man's night vision began to adjust to the surrounding room. The entity, who had transformed herself only two weeks before, again appeared to have changed form. To Turley, Henrietta's face seemed thinner and slightly matured from his place on the couch. In this instant, it occurred to him that his child specter resembled a pre-teen Brooke Shields as she appeared in the motion picture, *Pretty Baby*, some fifteen years earlier. "Why don't you come closer and join me on the couch," he suggested in the most tender tone he was capable of uttering. Only seconds passed before the spirit rose to its feet and moved toward him.

Turley's eyes were trained on the young woman's form as it raised itself up and onto the sofa. She took possession of the exact spot she had been flushed from twenty minutes earlier. He looked closely at her. In addition to her facial changes, the apparition appeared to have aged from less than two weeks earlier. He estimated that she was now slightly over five feet in height and long of limb. His best guess now placed her age at close to twelve, possibly even thirteen. Her transition into womanhood was about to commence, he reasoned. Now squarely seated on the sofa, Henrietta tucked her long, gangly legs under her and locked her eyes on him. Jonathan's thought process was careening out of control at this moment as he tried to again come to grips with his new reality. Somehow, he had fostered a relationship with a young woman from beyond the grave and this unnatural creature was sitting an arm's length from him in his living room. Involuntarily, he slid sideways and closer to the lovely, young creature and felt the need to caress her shoulder. She neither lurched away or showed any discomfort with the gesture.

"What year is it, Henrietta?" Turley asked. He had decided to ask the question days before.

"1861," she answered. Her response sent a chill through his entire body. His circumstances within the house were bending all notions of reality as he knew them. He stared long and hard at the child and again marveled at her loveliness. His mind flashed back to their first encounter and he was astonished by the change in her appearance. She appeared to have aged half a dozen years in only a few weeks, he thought. "I cannot find my mother, but I know she would never leave me alone with Mr. Wilson. Where could she be?" she asked, training her bewitching, dark eyes on Turley. He leaned forward and kissed the girl on the cheek. There was no warmth from her breath. His gesture sparked a rush of affection from the girl. She wrapped her arms around him and rested her head on his chest. "You'll stop Mr. Wilson if he tries to touch me again, won't you?" questioned the girl. He reached down and ran his fingers through the child's soft, silky hair.

"Of course, I will," he reassured her. The two sat in an embrace for a time, the man's mind and body now under the spell of his supernatural guest. However, his ethereal interlude was interrupted when Henrietta's head jutted up and turned in the direction of the hallway.

"I must hide," she insisted and scrambled to her feet. Jonathan, a willing prisoner of the trance he was under, was slow to react to the girl's imaginary crisis and remained anchored to the sofa. In the next second, she disappeared into the walls of the house. Five minutes after Henrietta's hasty departure, Jonathan climbed the stairs to his second story bedroom and retired for the night.

On a sunny, Saturday afternoon in November, Jonathan decided to take a stroll through the neighborhood. Besides the prospect of fresh air, he thought a change in scenery might help clear his mind of the lingering effects of the paranormal activity in the house. Hooking up with Ocean Avenue, he walked the distance to the open ocean before succumbing to the chill of a sea breeze. On the trek back to the house and within a stone's throw of his driveway, he met up with an Elm Street neighbor making repairs to his front fence. Turley made eye contact and the gentleman flashed him a civil smile. The gesture provided him with the impetus to initiate a conversation. Within seconds the subject of their respective properties was introduced. The man's eyes widened when Jonathan informed him that he was the new owner of the Bruckner House.

"I actually met the former owners of your house two or three years back. They were a couple of sisters from Massachusetts. I got the impression they were a little overwhelmed by the property...like they may have bitten off a little more than they could chew," he theorized. "How's it working out for you so far?" asked the man.

"So far, so good," answered Turley. He was not prepared to share any of his experiences with a total stranger.

"Now, you do know the history of the house, don't you?" Jonathan shrugged his shoulders.

"Not really," he confessed. The stranger seemed surprised.

"Well, like so many of the houses in this section of town, it was built early in the nineteenth century. It gained some notoriety back around the civil war when the woman of the house mysteriously disappeared. No one knew if she had run away or had been done in by the husband. The scandal made its way all the way down and into the Boston papers. A short time passed and then the husband and a daughter went missing. Anyway, the story was all people could talk about for a while and then along came the civil war and no one cared anymore."

"Do you, by any chance, remember the family's name?" questioned Turley.

"I want to say it was Wilson, but I wouldn't bet good money on it." Jonathan stared at the man, his mind processing the information. A slightly awkward lull fell over the conversation. Jonathan jumped in to fill the void.

"Well, I can't say I'm unhappy with the sister's decision to move away," he blurted out. His comment brought a contemplative expression to the neighbor's face.

"They were very unhappy there. I think the size of the house caused their minds to play tricks on them," he declared.

"In what way?"

"Noises. They both claimed they heard noises. In the end, I'm pretty sure that's what drove them out. God, I don't think they lived there any more than two months. They had to lose a small fortune," he declared. The neighborly conversation moved on to more mundane subjects like winter snow plowing and trash pickup before it broke up and Jonathan returned home. The walk back and forth to the sea had provided him with some valuable information, he reasoned. Somehow, one hundred and thirty years later, he was now dealing with the aftermath of the Wilson family's residence in the house.

On a Monday night in November, Jonathan stayed up and watched the nationally televised football game until well after midnight. Incredibly, by this time, he had accepted most of the house's paranormal activity. He had come to relax in the Bruckner House over the past six weeks. The presence in the attic had become more passive in his mind. For this reason, he avoided the third floor of the house, hoping to placate the spirit. In the case of Henrietta, he was more than happy to share the house with her. Truth be told, he was almost ashamed of the pleasure derived from having her physical attention on the sofa a week before. It had not been lost on Turley that, given the yearly progressions apparent in her last two manifestations, there was reason to believe she would be approaching womanhood on her next visit. He was fully aware of the foul thoughts now cultivated in his imagination but was equally mindful of the absence of any legal constraints on his actions.

At a half hour beyond midnight, Jonathan turned off the television and made his way up the stairway toward his bedroom. The second story hall was illuminated by nothing more than a low wattage bulb strategically placed near the landing. It was at the top of the flight of stairs that he felt an inexplicable pulse of fear pass through his stomach. It was purely intuitive, akin to the feeling of being watched when walking along a darkened path in the woods. He marched toward the door to his bedroom. Almost against his will, he glanced upward to the attic door. There, standing before the door, was the persona of a middle-aged woman. She stood motionless under a crown of disheveled hair. Her eyes were locked on him, her facial expression exhibiting the controlled resolve usually only witnessed on a battlefield. He felt his body grow rigid. Heart pumping feverishly, he scurried into the bedroom and slammed the door behind him. He dared not close his eyes. In his retreat downstairs a few minutes later, Turley noticed no evidence of the spirit on the attic stairwell. After due consideration, he slept in his car.

Jonathan moved his bed downstairs the following day, setting it up in the sitting room. He decided to keep an entire floor of the house as a buffer between him and the female entity occupying his attic. Just prior to Thanksgiving, the office landed a lucrative new client that placed demands on his time over the following weeks. On the weekend before Thanksgiving, he found himself hunkered down at his work table. It was nearly ten o'clock. A healthy fire sent warmth to even the far corners of the room while Jonathan was content to work with the light of a single, floor lamp. In an opposite corner sat the bed carried down from the second floor. Although engrossed in his work, he nonetheless found himself regularly scanning the room in search of any sign of Henrietta. From a nearby window, he detected the sound of droplets hitting glass. The raindrops would soon be snowflakes, he thought. Rubbing his tired eyes, he considered calling it a night. He glanced toward the fire and saw Henrietta posed in her usual position. With arms wrapped around her knees, she stared sadly in his direction. It was at that moment that he realized he had never seen the girl smile, let alone laugh. She rose to her feet and the sight of her set off his imagination. Her progression through childhood was nearing completion. Before the man stood an adolescent approaching physical perfection. The black hair cascading over her shoulders framed a pair of eyes that left him speechless. Under the dressing gown, he visualized her youthful, slender, teenage body. Turley was paralyzed in place as his paranormal guest closed the distance between them. Then, she was standing over him, her ethereal beauty sending his imagination careening out of control.

"You won't let him hurt me, will you?" she asked sorrowfully. "You're my friend and you'll protect me," she reiterated. He rose to his feet and took hold of the apparition, a phantom with form and substance. He ran his hands down her body until they rested on her buttocks. The voice of his conscience cried out from deep inside. but he chose to not heed it. Victimized in life and victimized in death," he thought. He had no control over his urges. He glanced toward the bed.

The two stood in an embrace.

"You won't let him hurt me," she repeated. He brought his lips in contact with the cool surface of her neck and tasted the flesh of the departed. He became excited and the specter made no attempt to pull away. It was at this precise moment that a third presence made itself known.

"Henrietta," called out a voice from the far corner of the room. The girl stiffened and looked over her shoulder.

"Momma," she cried back. Turley held tight but the young, female entity struggled to loosen his grip.

"I've come for you, my darling," called out the ghastly intruder. He peered over to see the entity residing in his attic standing by the far wall. She was clothed in a soiled, tattered dress, her hair disheveled in the same manner as before. The female specter reached out her arms to the girl. The beautiful creature in his embrace intensified her struggle while Jonathan tightened his grip. "I've come back for you. You'll come with me and leave this place forever," stated the haggard looking spirit. Her mother's words sent the youthful entity into a near hysterical rage as she further stepped up the struggle to free herself. In some bizarre way, the scuffle seemed to only intensify the state of arousal now controlling Turley. He tore at the child's dressing gown, conscious of the lack of any legal consequences. He had no fear of the female spirit standing across the room. His hand found the child's right breast and he squeezed her soft, cool flesh. She half turned back to him but did not cry out. It was at this moment that a severe pain tore through his rib cage. Turley drew in an agonizing breath and grabbed at his side. His grip on Henrietta was partially broken when his hand reached down to the source of his pain. He let out a terrible cry and gazed down at his wound. Through a fountain of spurting blood, he caught sight of the handle to his revered Hannibal Hamlin hunting knife. With one arm, he hung tight to the struggling spirit while she continued her efforts to break free of her tormentor. The blade burned inside of him while blood poured from the wound. The youthful spirit continued her battle to set herself free. Her exertions only amplified his pain. In a final ditch effort for freedom, Henrietta drove a knee into Turley's side. He cried out in pain, released his grip and slumped toward the floor. The child stood over the kneeling man for an instant, her feet standing in a shallow pool of his blood. In a final futile effort, Jonathan swiped at the girl's ankle. She avoided his hand and started across the room in the direction of the older, female spirit. Turley summoned all his strength and attempted to pull the knife from between his ribs. His effort was in vain. His fingers slid over the surface of the weapon's handle but failed to budge the blade. Blood now gushing from his mouth, he cried out to the young specter. The beautiful child failed to even glance back at him. She was already cradled in the protective arms of her mother. With the wound burning like fire in his side, he briefly thrashed against the inevitable and finally drew in a final, beleaguered breath. Jonathan Turley slumped to the floor, his face coming to rest in a warm pool of his own blood.

In the end, it was April Grant who called the police department and reported the question of Jonathan's whereabouts. Given the specifics of the man's death an autopsy was ordered. From the angle of the blade's entrance, it was determined that the wound was not self-inflicted. An examination of the premises showed no sign of forced entry, no sign of any prolonged struggle and the absence of any second party, fingerprint evidence that matched anything on file in criminal libraries. Neighbors reported not seeing anyone either arriving or leaving the property the night of the suspected murder. With no relatives or loved ones to stoke the fire of inquiry the probable homicide investigation soon went cold and was abandoned.

In the years to come, future owners of the Bruckner house reported no evidence or experience of paranormal activity.

About the Author

Thomas E. Coughlin is the author of the best-selling novel, Maggie May's Diary. He is a practicing certified public accountant and former radio announcer. He was born, raised and educated in Lowell, Massachusetts. He resides in Chester, New Hampshire.

If you enjoyed reading

Youthful Indulgence

by
Thomas E. Coughlin

Look for his other works of fiction

Maggie May's Diary

Brian Kelly: Route 1

The Odyssey of Sheba Smith

Obscene Bliss

Miss O'Malley's Maine Summer

Prey to the Butterfly

The Kellys of Wells, Maine

Wasted on the Young

The Path to Obsession